SOUTHERN ENCHANTED
SWEET TEA WITCH MYSTERIES BOOK TWENTY-THREE

AMY BOYLES

LADYBUGBOOKS LLC

CHAPTER 1

Of all the days and all the moments in my life, both good and bad, this one would go down in the history books as the worst.

It was after Christmas; winter was in full blast. But you know in the South we have really weird winters. It can be thirty degrees in January with a hot sun and then in February it can go all the way up to sixty-something degrees, then a day later the temperature will drop and we'll have a snowstorm. Everything will shut down.

And when I say everything, I mean all businesses. Nothing will be open for about a day. But by the next afternoon, it'll be sixty degrees again, the sun will be high in the sky, and the snow will melt.

But this day had nothing to do with snow. It had everything do with my shop, Familiar Place, where I matched witches to their pet familiars.

For those of y'all who don't know me, my name is Pepper Dunn Reign and I'm a witch. I live in the small town of Magnolia Cove, Alabama, with my husband, Axel, and our daughter, Gisela, or Gizzy for short.

That morning, I had walked to work along Bubbling Cauldron Road, and when I rounded a corner and laid my gaze on my shop, the world stopped.

The front windows had been bashed, leaving shards of sparkling glass glinting in the sun. The door was also broken; it sagged sadly from the frame. The sound of groaning hinges sent a shiver whipping down my spine.

My heart nearly halted. I stared at the store, unable to form a coherent thought. It's strange what happens to your brain in times of great stress—which this was.

A scream didn't force its way out of my throat. I didn't immediately reach for my phone to call anyone. Instead I charged toward the store. Not because I wanted to face whoever had done this, but because there were no signs of life coming from the shop.

My store was supposed to be filled with animals—birds, kittens, puppies, snakes, mice. Any creature that a witch could possibly need to help her wield her magic, I had it in stock, ready to be purchased.

So yes, I was afraid for my animals.

I picked my way over the broken glass and opened the door. It swayed out and then crashed to the ground. I jumped as both fear and anger bubbled in my gut.

Who had done this? Why had someone wrecked my life? None of the other shops had been touched. Just mine.

There was no doubt that I had enemies. There had been plenty of people I'd sent to prison. But that was because they'd committed some sort of crime. And others had tried to kill me. Some of them had wound up dead themselves. Did they have relatives who were now hunting me down, wanting to take from me what I'd taken from them?

My heart started to race even more than it already was, if you could imagine that. No. I could not let my anxiety and worry get ahold of me. I first had to go inside and make sure that none of the animals were hurt.

There was so much glass. What if…?

I shoved thoughts of harmed animals from my mind and stepped inside the store. Glass crunched under my feet. It appeared as if when the windows broke, the debris had gone in many different directions. The glass didn't just go inside; it was outside, too.

How was that even possible?

I picked my way into the heart of my shop and found that my creatures were gone. They'd either been taken or set free.

It was time to make a call. I found my phone in the bottom of my purse (the place where old tissues and ponytail holders went to die, I often joked) and dialed Axel.

"Hey, babe," he said in a sultry voice.

As much as I wished this was a casual call, there was nothing casual about what I had witnessed. "Something's happened at Familiar Place."

Alarm instantly filled his voice. "What?"

"There's been a break-in. All the animals are gone."

"I'll be right there. Get outside in case whoever did this is still there, waiting for you."

We hung up and I did as he said, stepping out to wait, the whole time wondering just who had done this and why. But also, where were the animals? Were they safe?

I pulled my coat tight as a wind sliced through me, and prayed with all my might that every creature was okay.

"THIS IS HOW SHE FOUND IT," Axel said a while later to Sheriff Mullins Rob, the new law in town.

Now Mullins Rob was not a pretty face. Not by a long shot. He wore a black patch over a missing eye and had a hook for a hand. Only one hook. He had another hand, luckily.

I'd jokingly referred to him as Sheriff Pirate when we'd first met. He'd been rough as sandpaper along the edges but was slowly coming around.

And right now Sheriff Rob's single eye was scouring the premises of Familiar Place as a crowd gathered outside. "And no one was here when you arrived?"

"No," I answered, shaking my head. "Every animal was gone."

"Interesting," he told me. "I need to find out if you were the only business hit, or if any of the others were affected as well."

I spotted Harry and Theodora from the shop next door to mine, Castin' Iron. I waved them over. "Did anyone break into y'all's shop last night?"

Harry scratched his head. "Let me think a minute."

Theodora smacked his chest. "You ain't got to think about it. No. Nobody broke in. Everything's exactly as it's supposed to be. 'Let me think a minute,'" she mumbled, mimicking her husband. "Harry, I swear, if you weren't old and ornery, I'd get rid of you."

He shrugged. I had a feeling they went through this argument a lot.

I winced at Mullins Rob. "I guess there weren't any other break-ins, or breakouts, whichever the case may be."

Mullins opened his mouth to say something as a new voice broke through the murmurs and whispers that filtered through the crowd.

"Out of my way. Coming through!" Betty waddled into the sea of witch and wizard spectators, elbowing them aside. "I said, move! That's my granddaughter's shop that's been attacked. She needs my help."

The crowd parted, though I had the feeling that if it had been up to them, none of them would have moved a muscle. They wouldn't even have blinked.

What tipped me off was the way they crossed their arms, fingernails digging into their biceps, or that they cinched closer together when Betty started shouting at them to move.

Even witches liked to have a front-row seat at a spectacle. They were sometimes a little possessive about it.

Anyway, the crowd released Betty from its hold like a leech letting go of warm flesh.

She glanced back at them and scowled. "All some people care about is getting their picture in the paper."

I shook my head. Did she really think there would be a big write-up in the local rag?

Next thing I knew, a reporter poofed onto the scene. I groaned. It wasn't just any reporter. This was Victoria Vshara. She was the worst. Always butting her nose into business that wasn't hers.

Well, I supposed that was what reporters did. But I had no interest in having my store be front-page news.

Victoria sidled like slime up to Mullins Rob. "Sheriff, what do you know so far about the break-in?"

I shot Axel a pleading look. He nodded and crossed to her. "Victoria, so good to see you. How about I tell you everything that I know?"

Which I knew would be nothing. But Victoria appeared confused. She slowly closed and opened her heavily lashed eyes (I'm not kidding when I say *heavily*—the lashes were so thick that I was surprised she didn't fall over from the weight of them).

"Oh, okay, Axel. Sure, if you have something to tell me. I'd love to hear everything." She licked her ball point pen and conjured up a notepad. "I'm ready."

Axel started talking, but I didn't hear what he said because Betty took charge of the situation. She pushed up her sleeves, pulled her pipe from her pocket, stuck it between her teeth and started puffing. Apparently it had been lit while in her clothing.

Talk about a fire hazard.

"What theories do you have, Sheriff?" she asked Rob.

He looked momentarily confused until I mouthed to him, *Just go with it.* Then he cleared his throat. "It seems no one saw the perpetrator."

She tapped her chin. "They didn't, huh? Any other stores vandalized?"

Theodora shouted, "Unless you count Harry's flatulence as vandalization, then no!"

The crowd laughed at that. Great. How had this break-in become a three-ring circus so quickly?

Betty strutted toward the front door. "Let me have a look."

Sheriff Rob cut her off. "I'm sorry, but as much as I hate to say it, if you go inside, you'll be destroying evidence, Betty. Now, your family has been good to me, very kind, very loyal and generous."

Had we, actually?

I supposed we'd offered friendship when Rob wasn't very deserving of it. Betty had invited him for dinner several times, and he had come. So I guess, maybe we had been kind, loyal and generous—to use his words.

But then he continued. If he'd just stopped there, everything would've been okay. But no, Sheriff Rob kept on a'blabbing. "But even though you've been all those things, I can't let you into that shop. It's a crime scene."

Betty's gaze raked over him as if he was a slug sitting on her shirt and she was about to flick him the heck off. "Listen, Sheriff, what you don't know is that I am a VIP in this town. My family has helped out with plenty, and I mean plenty of crime scenes. In fact, if it wasn't for us, half the criminals in this town would never have been caught."

"Right. I've read the previous sheriff's notes about that." Rob scrubbed a hand down the stubble peppering his cheeks. "Seems half of the time y'all just about got yourselves killed in the process."

"Details, details," she mumbled. "If you don't let me through, I'm going to force my way inside. Do you really want to have to arrest an old lady?" She leaned forward and whispered, "It won't look too good on you, being fairly new and all, ruffling an old lady's skirts, making her wig fall off, and letting the town see her bald."

"What?" Sheriff Rob recoiled. I almost recoiled, too. What in the world was Betty talking about? "No one here is going to accost you."

"That's what I thought." Betty hmphed. Then she lifted her nose high in the air (so high I was afraid she might trip on the curb) and strutted inside Familiar Place.

I shot Axel a look that asked, *Is she really doing this?*

He nodded. She was, indeed. That was when my husband disentangled himself from the nosy reporter's grasp. "I'm going in, too."

Sheriff Rob slapped his thighs. "Well, if half the town is going inside, then I am as well."

"Me too." I wasn't going to be left out alone. It was *my* shop, after all. "I'm right behind you."

We stepped inside, me walking in next to Axel, who placed a comforting arm around my shoulders. My stomach was a mess of butterflies, a wad of nerves. I curled inward, trying to protect myself from what we would uncover on the shelves and the floors of Familiar Place—besides glass, that was.

Betty charged in like a bulldog, peering into the cages. "Very interesting," she murmured as if she were Sherlock Holmes—an older, fatter, feminine version of the detective, that was.

She moved spryly over the glittering glass, making it pop and crackle under her feet. Good thing she wasn't wearing her house slippers.

After placing her hands on the bottom of the bird area and glancing inside the puppy's window, she whirled around, lifted a finger. "I know exactly what happened! Let me tell y'all all about it."

CHAPTER 2

I couldn't believe it. In less than two minutes Betty had the case solved. She knew who had broken into my store, who had released all my animals.

Great. All she had to do was spill the tea and I'd be out and about, gathering my puppies and kittens, bringing them back into the fold.

After all, if I didn't have animals to sell, then I didn't have a business.

She wasn't saying anything, which was super perplexing, as if she was waiting for me to hound her for information.

Oh, right. She probably was.

I rubbed my hands with glee. "All right, Betty. Lay it on us. Who did this?"

She grimaced. "I don't know *who* did it. All I said was that I know what happened."

Close enough. "Okay, then. What happened?"

"It started last night," she said mystically, and I immediately groaned.

Was she seriously going to milk all this for attention? Axel's hand on my shoulder tightened in support. I supposed the answer was yes, my grandmother was going to enjoy the limelight exactly as long as she could.

Betty continued. "Last night, these creatures were freed from their cages. I would have expected magic to have been involved, but I don't think so. I believe whoever did this entered and manually let all the creatures go."

I frowned. "So this was, like, a normal robbery?"

"Yes."

I glanced up at Axel. "Does that sound right?"

"There's no trace of magic. She's right about that. I don't feel any residual power running through the air."

"So…what happened?" I asked, now thoroughly confused. If magic wasn't a part of the robbery, then what did occur? "This is a magical town. Why would someone break in, steal my animals and do so without using any type of power? How did the windows get broken if magic wasn't involved?"

"I believe whoever did this flew into a rage," she explained.

A rage. Like, someone charged into my store, got all ticked off, emptied the cages and then smashed the windows? This wasn't a big city. That kind of stuff didn't happen here.

It was taking a minute to wrap my head around this. "Let me get this straight: someone magical entered nonmagically, released all my animals and then got angry and took a baseball bat to the windows and door?"

She shrugged. "It might not have been a baseball bat."

I dropped my head into my hands. "I don't understand any of this. First, I don't get why anyone would wreck the place."

Axel cleared his throat.

I took the hint. "Okay, maybe I've put a few people behind bars. But it wasn't because I broke the law. *They* broke the law, not me." I shot my husband a pleading look. I don't know why I was pleading; it was just how the expression filled up my face. "You think someone did this out of revenge?"

"Why else?" He walked around. I cringed with every glass-crunching step he took. "Why else would someone have targeted you, this store, your animals? They wanted to take away from you the most important thing in your life."

The animals were important to me, very important, but they weren't the most important things in my life. There was my family—Axel and our baby, Gisela.

Oh no. What if whoever had struck here had done something to the baby? What if they'd stolen her? She was at Betty's, but Betty was standing in front of me pretending to be *Sherlocka Holmes*, Sherlock's less famous little sister.

No, of course Sherlock Holmes didn't have a sister.

Okay, maybe Enola was his sister. I didn't know. I hadn't read any of the books. I only saw that one Netflix movie that starred the girl from *Stranger Things* playing Enola.

Anyway, my daughter!

"Betty, where's Gizzy?"

"She's with Amelia."

Oh, good. That meant she was safe.

"Sherman was going over to the house so that they could run over details about the wedding."

Which meant—disaster.

Amelia was getting married—*finally*, according to her. Apparently she'd been chomping at the bit for Sherman to propose. Well, he had, which meant that Amelia's world was now filled with planning said wedding. She'd even dragged out a big photo-type album that she kept hidden under her bed. It was filled with pictures of headless women in bridal gowns. Actually, they weren't headless. Amelia had taped her head to the top of every dress after she decapitated the original models.

But that wasn't all that was in the book. There were swatches of materials, venue choices (one was even the Conjuring Caves—who had a wedding in a cave?), menu options depending on what time of day the ceremony was held, and also color combinations so that she could choose the best hues for her wedding (which depended on the season, of course).

But my point was, Amelia was distracted. I didn't even know if Sherman had seen the book, but if he hadn't, she would keep him busy for a good two hours going through all the pages and explaining what every picture was about.

Trust me, I knew. I'd already lived it and had just about fallen asleep during our discussion.

I almost wished it was Cordelia, my other cousin, getting married instead. She would probably just elope to Witch Vegas or something, which in my opinion was a thousand times better than heaving out a Barbie book full of nuptial ideas.

Not that I was judging.

All right, I was judging. But I was doing my best *not* to judge. It was just so hard when the book was a good three inches thick and easily weighed as much as a baby.

A baby!

Gisella! I had to make sure that she was safe. My gaze darted to Axel. "If someone wanted to hurt me, they wouldn't stop at just releasing my animals. They would go after my family."

His face paled. Actually paled. Axel was as tough as his name—tougher, actually. Half werewolf, half wizard, he was all man—*very* manly and did manly things and even looked manly when he did those things. (Like chopping wood. He looked very testosterone-ish when he did that.)

But now he looked worried. To Betty he said, "She's at your house?"

"Yes."

Axel strode over to me with bone-crushing steps. I swore the glass popping beneath his feet turned to dust under his weight. He took my hand, and magic enveloped us.

It was a strong, emotion-filled power that circled me. "Take two steps," he ground out, "and we'll be in Betty's living room."

Oh, this was new magic. But there was no time to be razzle-dazzled by it. I tightened my grip on his hand and nodded.

We took two steps together. Familiar Place vanished, and we stood in Betty's living room. The Christmas decorations were all gone, though a couple of potted poinsettias were placed on tables as if to remind us that Christmas would return in ten months.

But who was counting?

Amelia sat on the couch with Sherman beside her. *The book* was opened and resting on both of their laps. Yes, it was so big that one lap couldn't even hold it. It spilled over onto any unsuspecting victim who happened to be sitting beside Amelia.

Only in this case, that victim was Sherman.

And he looked like it, too. His eyes were all glassed-over and his head was down. It looked as if he'd fallen asleep while studying pictures of three- and four-tiered wedding cakes.

Uh-oh. Groom better sit up before Amelia became a bridezilla.

"Pepper, Axel!" Amelia rose, obviously seeing the distress in our faces. The book slid onto Sherman lap's, hitting him hard in the crotch. He did his best not to double over, but he still squeaked out in pain. "What's wrong?"

"Where's Gizzy?" I asked.

"She's upstairs, sleeping," my cousin told us. "But what's wrong?"

Axel and I sprang up the stairs. "Her crib's in Betty's room," I said.

He led me straight inside. We rushed to the crib and found a sleeping Gizzy. Drool trickled from one side of her mouth, pooling onto her blankie (decorated with witches and cats—a gift from Betty) that she clutched in her chubby hand.

I exhaled a gust of air. "Thank goodness." I gently placed a hand on her head. "She's okay."

Axel nodded, but his mouth was set in a firm line. "We'll let her rest."

I followed him downstairs, my heart still thumping so hard I thought it might leap from my chest. Gizzy was safe. The relief I felt was almost impossible to describe. It was like a giant whale had been sitting on me and when I saw her, the whale vanished. Cold dread that I'd never known had literally taken over my body at the simple thought that Gizzy might have been stolen.

Also anger. If someone had taken her, I would've stopped at nothing to get her back.

Okay, all right. She was safe, so there was no point in me creating fanciful situations out of thin air.

But still, I would have harmed anyone who would do such a thing.

When we got back downstairs, Amelia was waiting for us. Sherman was standing too, though a bit hunched over, and the book was lying closed on the couch, as far away from where Sherman had been sitting as it could have been.

I understand that move, buddy, I wanted to tell him. But it wasn't going to help because as soon as we were gone, Amelia would just go right on over, open the book to where they left off and finish giving him the tour of her creation—down to the breath mints she thought would be good to hand out at the end of the reception.

I was not kidding.

"Everything okay?" Amelia asked.

"It's fine," Axel said.

"What happened?" she quizzed us. "Why did you come in like that, all worked up?"

I raked my fingers through my cinnamon and honey locks. "Familiar Place was broken into."

"I know, that's why Betty left." Amelia's worried gaze darted from Axel to me. "What's that got to do with Gizzy?"

"We were afraid that whoever had done that to Pepper might have also been targeting our family," Axel growled.

I patted his arm and gave him a look that said it was okay. We were all fine. No one in the room was the enemy.

"Oh," Amelia replied, not seeming to have noticed Axel's tone. "I hope that doesn't happen."

My phone rang. Betty's name lit up the screen. "Hello?"

Her voice was nearly impossible to make out. "Hmph, hmph, hmph," she said.

I rolled my eyes. "Do you have your phone upside down? Turn it the other way. I can't hear you when it's not right."

"I said," she replied, sounding crystal clear, "have you found Gizzy? Is she okay?"

"She's fine. Just asleep." I found myself glancing at Axel, who still looked ready to slug someone. "We'll be back in a few minutes."

"Take your time," she consoled me. "This was an attack on you, on our family. I'm not going anywhere."

"Okay," I said weakly.

"And Pepper," my grandmother told me, sounding tough, "we're going to find the son of a gun who did this."

"We will."

In my tone I tried to convey that I believed that, that I was ready to take on a fight, but to be honest, this entire thing had been exhausting. The day had barely started, and it was already a disaster. Could it really get any worse?

Scratch that—of course it could get worse. It always did. Experience had taught me that.

I hung up the phone and gave Axel a weak smile, which reflected exactly how my stomach felt—wimpy and weak, fairly queasy. It was also rolling quite a bit.

Perhaps it would have been better to focus on other things instead of my gut.

"So"—I tried to sound chipper—"what do we do now?"

"You," my husband told me, sounding very stern, "will take Gizzy home and stay there. I'm going back to Familiar Place to help with the investigation. Perhaps someone else saw or heard something. There may be clues that we've overlooked."

The way he said that I was going home stabbed me. I wanted to help; I needed to be in the middle of the melee. But Axel was right. First and foremost, I needed to see to Gizzy.

But she was safe with Amelia and Sherman, who was a blacksmith, which more than likely meant that he had some sort of magical piece of steel on him at any given time.

I had no idea if that was true, but it seemed highly likely.

Sherman, seeming to sense my hesitation, replied, "I'll stay here, Axel. If you think it would be okay for Pepper to return to Familiar Place. I mean, all your animals gone? Sounds like someone worked very hard to hurt you."

Axel exhaled a hard breath. "All the more reason for her to stay somewhere safe. And to look after Gizzy."

"I won't feel safe at the house by myself," I pleaded.

"And I've got my sword here—it'll cut through most spells." From behind the couch, Sherman pulled a broadsword. It was about three feet long with a guard as wide as two hands. How had I not noticed the monstrous thing before? "Just finished making it. Tried it out on a few spells. I've got high hopes for it."

Axel looked torn. On the one hand, he wanted to keep me safe. On the other, he knew what I was saying about the house—that being alone there wasn't going to do me or Gizzy any good.

"It's a big weapon," I hinted to Axel. "I bet it could cut through a person, if not a spell."

"Oh, it won't cut a person," Sherman argued.

Sherman, you are not helping.

"I'll be here," Amelia added. "We'll bring Gizzy down in a minute."

Axel's face remained expressionless, which meant he was considering it. After a moment he finally said, "All right. Come on. Let's see what other clues we can muster up."

It took everything I had not to do a fist pump. That was one victory for me and one for the mystery vandal.

I prayed the vandal wouldn't be hard to take down, but I had a feeling that in asking for that, I was biting off more than I could chew.

CHAPTER 3

There weren't any clues to be found at the scene of the crime. By the time we returned, Sheriff Rob and his crew had used their magical abilities and searched for any threads on clothing, fingerprints, whatever they could find that would lead them to the culprit, but nothing was to be unearthed.

It was, in a word, heartbreaking. After the police and Betty had gone, leaving Axel and myself to clean up the mess, I grabbed a broom and started sweeping.

I didn't have it in me to use magic to clean up the glass. Then everything would be fixed in a moment, and I wouldn't have the luxury of taking the time to hear the glass scratch the floor as I swept it into a dustpan.

"You're really wanting to torture yourself, aren't you?" Axel said.

"You don't have to stay here. I can clean up myself."

He shot me a dark look. "I'm not leaving."

"Good. You can hang out with me and my misery." He laughed, but what I'd said wasn't meant to be funny. "I wasn't trying to humor you." He took the broom from my hands. "I was using that and would appreciate having it back."

"Not until we have this conversation."

"What conversation?" And why couldn't he just give the darned thing back to me? Why was my husband being difficult? Was it fun to torture me? Kick me while I was already down? "What do we need to talk about?"

"Where do you think all your animals are?"

"I don't know." I lifted my arms and then let them slump to my sides. "Dead? Captured by some person who must've wanted to start their own familiar shop but didn't have the funds? In Canada? Oh my goodness. Those are Southern animals. How are they going to get along in Canada?"

He winked at me. "Full of Yankees, isn't it?"

"Oh my gosh, it is!"

He chuckled. "You're beginning to sound like Betty."

"But it's true. Those animals are Southern. They don't do well in the cold. They probably won't do well in the heat, either. They're used to a man-made, manufactured environment, one where the air-conditioning's on in the summer and the heat is blasting in the winter. They'll never make it in a place that gets down to thirty below zero."

I didn't know if it got that cold in Canada, but it sounded good. Surely some parts were that frosty. After all, Canada was really close to the North Pole.

Axel placed his hands on my shoulders and pulled me into a hug. "It's okay. Calm down."

"But they're…they're out there. Alone. With some crazy person who's got them trapped in small boxes while they're sitting in the back of a pickup truck somewhere, heading north, and I'm sure they're all afraid and worried and wondering where Preggers is, even though I'm not pregnant but they still call me that."

He pulled me into a hug and pressed his lips to my hair. "Why do you think whoever broke in here broke all the windows? They didn't have to."

I clutched Axel's shirt and pressed my nose into the space just below his neck, where his scent was strongest. I inhaled and exhaled. With every fill of my lungs, his bouquet trickled up my nose, offering comfort where none could be found otherwise.

"Hmm?" he pressed. "Why was that?"

Oh, right. He'd asked me a question. What had it been, again? "Why'd the thief break the windows? I don't know, just to be a jerk?"

"I don't think so."

"You don't, huh? Then why'd he do it? Not that I'm trying to be sexist and immediately blame all of this on a man, but I don't think a woman would've been that violent."

"I don't, either." Axel stroked my hair. "I'm fairly certain it was a man, and I'm also fairly certain that he didn't steal your animals."

I jerked back and stared up at him in surprise. "You are? Well, what else would he have done? Why would he have done this? Do you mean to tell me that whoever is behind this vandalism broke in, freed my animals, destroyed the windows and then went about their merry way?"

"Yes, I do."

I stopped. My heart thundered in my chest. The sound of rushing blood hummed in my ears. I searched Axel's eyes, trying to see if he was joking or not.

But the look on his face said it all—he was deadly serious.

Right. Well, maybe not deadly. After all, this wasn't exactly a life-and-death situation. But he did look serious as a heart attack.

"But why would someone have done that?" I questioned. "Why go to all that trouble for nothing?"

"Maybe it wasn't trouble for them." He released his hold on me and scrubbed a hand down his cheek. "But did you see one crate, one scrap of wood that could've come from a carrier?"

"Maybe he didn't house them in wood. Maybe he used plastic. It's a lot lighter."

"It is, but I don't think so. No. I think this is a story of someone doing this to spite you."

"But, but...they could have carried them off in steel? Had steel containers."

Why was I working so hard to convince myself that the perpetrator had taken my animals away? Was it because the alternative meant—

I gasped. "You think the animals are nearby, don't you?"

Axel nodded. "I do. That's why I don't think you should be in here, sweeping up this mess. We should be out there, searching for them."

"Oh my gosh. I didn't even think of that. This whole time I just figured that whoever had done this had stolen them, that he'd taken my animals to resell, start his own familiar business at the expense of mine."

"I don't think so." Axel's blue eyes darkened to the color of a stormy sea. "And the longer we stand here, cleaning—"

"The farther away they're going." I clapped his shoulder. "Well, what are we waiting for? Let's go find my animals!"

∾

SEARCHING for my animals and finding them were two polar opposite things. In my mind, searching and finding were one. We would search. Then we would find.

But the reality turned out to be very, very different.

I stood on the sidewalk along Bubbling Cauldron Road. I'd literally walked about twenty paces from the inside of my store to outside. "Okay, where do we start?" I asked Axel.

"Well, let's think. If you were an animal, where would you go?"

"Some place with climate control," I joked. Actually, it wasn't a joke. I would find a place with heat because even though the sun shone brightly, it was cold, very cold.

He frowned. I supposed my answer had not been entirely sincere. Axel, my husband, the love of my life, corrected me. "If you were an animal, wouldn't you want to go where other animals might be? Wouldn't you feel the draw of other creatures?"

Oh, that was a good point. I hadn't considered that. "Yes," I honestly said, "I would want to be around my kind. If I were a cat, I would want to find a crazy cat lady."

He shook his head. "You are not helping."

I shrugged. "What? I would want to find someone like that because obviously they would take care of me. They would hug me and squeeze me."

"And let the other cats take you out when the old lady wasn't looking."

I grimaced. "You have quite the imagination."

"Touché."

Well, I guessed that was true. I did have quite an imagination at times. But clearly, at the moment, my mind wasn't helping me to figure out what had happened to my animals.

Think, Pepper.

I closed my eyes and focused. If all the kittens and puppies were suddenly free, at first they would have been scared. They wouldn't have known what to do. A person would've raced into their home and destroyed it. They would have scattered when they reached the outside, going in opposite directions. But they didn't stay here. They didn't return to Familiar Place, which would have been somewhat *familiar* to them.

Why?

The wheels in my mind kept turning and turning and turning. Animals worked on smell more than sight. They would've allowed their noses to lead them. What would have smelled comforting?

Not a home where a witch or wizard lived. No. That wouldn't have been where the animals would've gone. They would have wanted to search out a place that reminded them of what they were—animals.

My eyelids popped up. "I've got it!"

Axel shot me an amused look. I had the feeling he enjoyed making me do mental gymnastics. "You've got what?"

"The location of my creatures!" I grabbed his arm and started tugging him across the street. "They're in the Cobweb Forest."

CHAPTER 4

*I*f the Cobweb Forest was downright creepy at night, it wasn't much better during the day. The trees had a thing about them that was disturbing—they liked to pull up their roots and move when no one was looking, which could make things a bit disorienting if you were trying to, say, find your way out of the woods.

But luckily Axel, given that he was half werewolf, had an amazing sense of smell, one that could help us find our way out if we had to.

Oh, we also had magic. That could actually come in handy, too. So you know, it wasn't like we would get completely lost in the forest. We would find our way home eventually.

"Where do you think they would be?" I whispered as we approached the trees. They were spaced close, pulled together as if they didn't want us to enter.

I swallowed a knot in my throat. They *didn't* want us in there, right? I wasn't imagining things. Trees weren't sentient. Okay, they could bark like dogs, move and even spit their pine needles at me (as I discovered not too long ago), but they couldn't actually *think*, could they?

Impossible.

Axel exhaled a low breath. "You ready?"

"As ready as I'll ever be."

"I'll be able to smell them," he told me. "If we get close."

A gusty breeze blew past us, picking up my hair and slapping it across my face. Huh. I hoped that wasn't a foretelling of what was to come.

You know, I'd end up witch-slapped or something stupid like that.

Axel gave my hand a squeeze and we entered. I swear that the sky darkened as soon as we crossed some strange, imaginary line that separated the forest from the rest of Magnolia Cove.

The trees bent in the wind, their leaves shuddering and their branches quivering. But that was the only sound. There wasn't the yip of a puppy or the mew of a kitten to be heard.

But sometimes squirrels sounded like kittens. Have y'all ever noticed that? They make some sort of call, probably a distress call that sounds almost just like a cat.

But anyway, I wasn't going to be fooled by a squirrel pretending to be a kitten.

"Which way should we go?" I asked Axel.

He paused before saying, "This way."

I followed him through the dense foliage. After a few minutes we came to a fork in the forest.

"I don't remember this," I murmured.

"It changes; you know that." Axel paused before leading us down a path to the left. "Come on."

If it had been up to me, I would have gone right. But you know, he was my husband, and he was also the one who could smell like a wolf. So…happy marriage and all that.

We followed the trail, and I swore that the canopy of trees were tightening around us, corralling us, almost, to keep to the trail and not even consider wandering off.

I clutched Axel's hand, doing my best to keep a straight face, but I still shivered nonetheless.

"You okay?" he asked.

"I'm fine. It's just that this place gives me the creeps."

"Oh, just this one? Or the entire forest?" he asked sarcastically.

I elbowed his ribs. "The whole place. Sometimes it's spookier than others."

"It certainly seems to have its own personality, doesn't it?"

I couldn't agree more. "That, it does."

We'd been walking a ways when the trees started to become more sparse. The path widened, and before us sat a cabin.

Woodsmoke poured from the chimney, and a stack of logs was piled up along the side of the building. Someone lived in the Cobweb Forest?

Who would live out here? The place was creepy, strange. The trees moved. The entire forest seemed to breathe with a life of its own—and I didn't think that it particularly cared for interlopers.

"Do you know who owns that cabin?" I asked Axel.

"No. Why would I?"

I shrugged. "Because you're a werewolf and you're king of your clan. You know pretty much everything that goes on in this town, so I thought you might know who would be insane enough to live out in the boonies, in a crazy haunted forest. I mean, doesn't a giant spider live out here somewhere? In one of the caves?"

"Someone's been reading too much Harry Potter again," he teased.

"Ha, ha. Very funny. But I'm serious."

"It wouldn't surprise me if there was, but I don't think 'giant spider' is on the list of creatures that the forest houses."

"If you say so."

He nodded firmly. "I do."

I stared at the house, uncertain what to do next. "Your nose led us in this direction, right?"

"It did."

"Well, should we knock and ask whoever answers if they've seen a group of baby animals? Some birds?"

"I don't see why not."

Axel strode toward the house, and fear clutched my heart. What if whoever lived inside was crazy? What if they were an ax murderer?

If so, I was sending my husband to his doom.

Not wanting Axel to be hurt, I scurried up to him and plopped myself by his side just before he knocked.

He smirked. "Worried I was going to be devoured by a man-eating turtle or something?"

"No. Yes. Does it matter? I'm here to keep you safe."

He smiled and rapped on door. A moment later it opened and a man with smooth blond hair answered. His flannel shirt was open all the way to the bottom and pulled back a little, revealing abs cut from diamond—or steel, something hard like that.

This guy's abs gave Axel's a run for their money.

Not that I was staring. I was so not staring.

Oh no. I was staring.

I quickly glanced to the ceiling.

"How do you do?" he said, all polite like. It must've been his way of disarming people who came to his door. You know, show off his abs and then give a lady a friendly smile before he sucks the life out of her.

He did live in the Cobweb Forest. That was fairly suspicious, or *sus*, as the kids said.

Axel thrust out his hand. "Name's Axel Reign."

"The werewolf?" The man's brows shot to the sky. "Out here in the forest?"

"My wife and I are on business, looking for some creatures."

The man's green eyes swiveled to me and then back at Axel. "Come on in."

Did we really want to go in? What if the man *was* the giant spider? Like, he turned into the creature or something? I know that I was being dramatic, but I didn't understand why anyone would choose to live in the Cobweb Forest. Either he was crazy, or he was...crazy. There were no other explanations.

"Name's Ross Priester," he told us when we were inside his terribly normal-looking cabin.

"Like the Priester's store that's on the way to the beach?" I asked.

Axel shot me a glance that said, *Really? You want to ask the man about food?* But I shrugged. That place was practically famous for their pecan logs. Plus, the building was huge and it was in the middle of nowhere off interstate I-65. Half of the Southeast and the Midwest traveled by it on their way to Gulf Shores every summer.

I didn't think the line of questioning was too far off brand, no.

Ross answered quickly. "I'm no relation to them."

I shot Axel a replying look that said, *See? It doesn't hurt to ask.*

"Would you like some tea? Coffee?" Ross asked.

"Tea would be great," I replied as Axel said, "No thanks."

We stared at one another. "We've been out in the cold for a while," I told him.

He relented. "I'll take whatever you've got on hand."

"Sure," Ross said, moseying over to the kitchen cabinets and not bothering to button his shirt, I noticed. Perhaps walking around with his shirt open was Ross's look. Like, some women wore the same earrings every day because they didn't want to have to think too hard about what to decorate their ears with. It sort of gave them a "look."

Okay, maybe it didn't give them a look, but you know what I mean.

Perhaps Ross's look was walking around with his shirt open. In the middle of winter.

Or every day in the summer, too.

He talked while he brewed the tea. "You might think it's strange that my wife and I would live out here."

Axel surveyed the house while Ross spoke. He was being all detective-ish while this nice man was fixing us a drink.

I decided that perhaps I should have been more detective-ish as well, so I started perusing the books in his bookshelf. They were all really boring, about building with wood and construction and yawn, things I had no interest in reading about.

"Your wife lives here?" Axel asked, repeating what Ross had said.

"Yeah, she's out, though. Be back later."

Framed pictures of a beautiful woman with flowing black hair littered the living room. If that was Ross's wife (and I was pretty sure she was), then she was gorgeous.

The kettle hissed, and Ross poured three cups of tea. He came back and handed me a cup. I did my best not to stare at his abs as I took it. Which was hard because I had to look down to take the cup, but had to remind myself to keep my gaze on the porcelain and not allow it to wander.

It was harder than I thought it would be.

But when we all had our cups, we sat in the open living room, which didn't have much furniture—a couch and a recliner. Just enough for the two people who lived in the cabin.

"You'll have to excuse the mess," Ross said, pointing to a stack of papers, "but we don't get many visitors out here."

Axel blew on the steaming liquid. "Yes. You were saying something about that before, you living in the Cobweb Forest. Why is that?"

Ross ran his hand through his thick locks, a sheepish expression on his face. "Well, my wife and I believe that being close to nature is important. We considered moving into town, but one day we were exploring the area and found this forest. So we built a house."

"With magic?" Axel asked.

Ross shook his head, frowning. "I don't use much magic. My wife doesn't, either. We believe in being minimalist with our talents. If we don't have to use magic, we won't. It's a tool, not an answer to every possible problem that presents itself to us."

What blasphemy!

I was only joking. "So," I said slowly, trying to wrap my head around what it was exactly that Ross was saying, "you mean to tell us that you built this house with your hands because you could."

He nodded. "Ellen and I have found that magic only brings on problems. The less we use it, the less problems we tend to have."

"Oh, I thought it solved problems," I replied. "At least it has for me."

"That's good for you," he said. "But our experience has been different."

His tone was almost a warning. Realizing that steering away from this topic was probably a good idea, I said, "The reason we're here is because we're searching for some things."

"Animals, to be exact," Axel explained.

"How can I help?" Ross said, looking like he honestly wanted to give us a hand.

I cleared my throat. Here went nothing. "I own a familiar shop in town, Magnolia Cove."

He nodded impatiently. Of course he knew which town I lived in. It wasn't as if there were dozens of magical villages nearby.

"This morning," I told him, "I discovered that my shop had been broken into and all the animals were gone, missing. We're here in the forest searching for them, and we thought that maybe you or your wife had seen them. I'm not talking about strange creatures—kittens and puppies, mostly, though there are some exotic birds. I'm worried about their safety and only want to bring them back to the store. Have you spotted any?"

Ross thought about it for a moment, a really long moment, before answering, "No, I haven't seen or heard anything. I was trying to remember if I'd heard any kittens or puppies, but besides the birds, I haven't seen anything. I'm sorry, I wish that I could say differently."

"Maybe your wife's spotted them?" I asked hopefully.

"Well, I wouldn't know. She won't be back until tonight."

"Tonight?" I said, unable to hide my surprise. Did she go out in search of food or something? Were they foragers as well as off-grid people? "Is she in town? Maybe we'll run into her in Magnolia Cove."

"She's seeing her aunt," Ross explained. "The older woman needs help during the day. So Ellen won't return until after sunset."

I shot Axel a hopeful look. "Maybe we can come by then and talk to her."

"No need." Ross smiled kindly. "I'll ask her and if she has seen them, she can call you. Maybe you can leave your number."

"Sure," Axel said, rising. "I'll be happy to."

What? He didn't want to give open-shirt Ross my digits? Was Axel jealous of a little man flesh? If he was, I would be teasing him about this for sure. No way would he get out of a little ribbing.

Axel wrote his number on a slip of paper that Ross found in the kitchen, and we headed for the door. "Thank you for your help," Axel said.

Ross draped one arm over the doorframe as we stood outside to say goodbye. He rubbed a hand down his chest. This guy was either terribly unselfconscious or he simply liked everyone to look at him and think sexy thoughts.

I didn't know the answer but had a feeling that my husband would have a sound opinion about him once we left.

"Thank you for the tea," I told him.

"Come back anytime," Ross said. "Maybe next time you'll get to meet my wife."

We said goodbye and walked off. Axel started heading back into the woods, but I stopped him. "Why're we returning the way we came? Shouldn't we keep going?"

He shook his head. "No. The faint whiff of animal scent that I got ended here."

My feet were suddenly stuck in place. "It stopped here?"

Axel's glance flicked back to the house. "That's right. Here, at Ross's home."

CHAPTER 5

That night I didn't sleep very soundly. I tossed and turned until morning. It felt that every hour I was up, checking the clock to see what time it was.

Eventually dawn broke and a new day began. Axel cheerfully made breakfast. He even passed me extra jelly beans to put into my sweet tea that morning. He must've sensed that I was off, that everything was wrong.

Gizzy was her normal happy self. She was such a gleeful baby, just an absolute joy to be around. I dropped her off at Betty's and did not stay to chat.

My grandmother had wanted to talk, but I was depressed. There wasn't another way to describe it. I was absolutely saddened by the fact that my animals were gone, which meant that I would have to rebuild my business from scratch.

Actually, from less than scratch. I'd have to create it from nothing. Which meant there was a lot of work for me to do.

I walked to work hoping that the fresh air would help, but it didn't. The only thing it did was to make me sink even deeper into my thoughts.

I considered what Axel had said—that the animal smell had ended at Ross's home. What did that mean? I hadn't seen any of my animals.

There wasn't a big barn behind the cabin where they could have been hiding.

Perhaps the scent trail ended simply because it ended. Or maybe Axel's sense of smell was a little off.

Don't tell him I said that.

Of course, that was unlikely. There wasn't anything wrong with Axel's smell. Maybe the animals had made it to the cabin and then they'd vanished into thin air.

Right.

But Ross hadn't seemed like he was holding anything back. He'd been as honest as he could have been.

That could only mean that his wife held answers that he didn't. Perhaps she knew the whereabouts of the animals. It would be worth checking on, talking to her about.

The only problem was, I didn't have her number.

That wasn't much of a problem, to tell the truth. I could figure something out.

Those thoughts were filtering through my head when I reached my store. All life immediately drained from me. There was magical yellow police tape strung across the door, but all the broken glass had been repaired.

"What the…?"

"He came and fixed it last night."

I turned around and spotted Harry cleaning his eyeglasses. "Who did?"

He looked through the lenses, frowned and wiped them again with a cloth. "Your husband."

"Axel?"

"Do you have another one?"

I chuckled. "No, of course not. But he came here?"

"Saw him myself."

"Well, I'll have to call Axel and thank him," I said, feeling chipper. "I appreciate you telling me."

"I'm surprised you didn't know," Harry said. "It all happened around dinnertime."

I frowned. Dinnertime? But Axel was home with me at dinner. He couldn't have been here, unless…it wasn't him.

My thoughts went sideways. Wait. Before I started working mental gymnastics, perhaps I needed to make sure that what Harry said was right. "Are you sure it was around dinner?"

"Oh yeah," he told me. "I waved at him and everything. He even said hello. Happened when I was shutting down the shop. The sun had already set, but there were lights on in the shop. There was no mistaking him."

This was a problem—like a real problem. Axel had most definitely been with me last night. He had not been anywhere near my shop. There were a thousand possibilities—okay, not a thousand, but a handful.

Perhaps not even that. Maybe only one or two.

But anyway, the first was that Harry was flat out wrong. That he'd mistaken someone else for my husband. I mean, Harry was standing before me cleaning his glasses. It was possible that perhaps the store light had gotten in his eyes and he wasn't able to see correctly. Total possibility.

But he'd spoken to Axel. Besides, who else could it have been?

Adam, that was who.

Oh. Don't tell me that y'all have forgotten about Adam, Axel's twin brother?

Adam was currently in prison, which was where I was certain that he still was.

Wasn't he?

What if he'd escaped and we hadn't been notified? What if he'd gotten out…and his first act as a free man was to fix my shop?

Okay, wow. That didn't make any sense. Why would a known criminal, someone who'd lived their life doing bad deeds, suddenly decide to do something nice?

Because they were trying to take over their brother's life, that was why.

My heart skidded to a stop. Was it possible? Could Adam have broken out of jail and instead of creating his own life, he'd decided to steal his brother's? What if he was tracking down Axel right now, ready to jump him and take what Adam believed was rightfully his?

Whoa. I needed to calm down. I didn't even know if Adam was out of prison. He was probably locked away tight in a cell doing a gazillion push-ups a day.

But what if he wasn't? What if he was free, and we just hadn't heard anything about it because the prison was trying to sweep the escape under the rug?

With my heart rate spiking, I told Harry to have a good day and scurried inside the all too empty Familiar Place. I didn't even take a moment to enjoy how cleaned up and beautiful the place was. All I could think about was that there was a dangerous criminal on the loose, one that was trying to usurp my family for his own.

Oh no. What if Adam had found his own Pepper while in prison? What if he'd met a woman who looked just like me and they'd escaped together and were now on their way here, to kill me and take my child for their own?

I sucked down several gulpfuls of air and told myself to get a grip. First, I had to confirm that Adam was in prison. That would be easy. A simple phone call was all it would take. In less than three minutes my fears would be squashed, and I'd be laughing at myself for being so ridiculous.

Adam, free? So silly of me. Then Axel and I would have a big laugh about it at dinner. I'd tell him how I got myself all worked into a tizzy over nothing, and he'd chuckle at how dramatic I was. For once I'd totally agree with him because I *was* being crazy dramatic.

I laughed to myself as I pulled my phone from my pocket and searched out the number for the prison, which was almost beneath my feet, by the way. The cave system that ran below the earth was not far from Magnolia Cove and housed the magical prison, Witcheroo. Was I ever worried about my safety? No. Those prisoners weren't going anywhere.

Or so I believed.

Anyway, I located the number and dialed it. A gruff man's voice came on the line. "Witcheroo."

He sounded none too pleased to be answering the phone, but who could blame him? He was a guard at a prison. It wasn't like it was a happy place to work.

But nonetheless, I attempted to sound cheerful. "Hello, this is

Pepper Reign. I was calling to confirm that you have a prisoner there... um, in stock."

Ugh, was saying *in stock* even right? But I didn't know how else to phrase it. What was I supposed to say? *Do you have a particular person locked up?*

Oh, right. I should have used the word *incarcerated*. Lucky for me, the guard didn't miss a beat.

"Who are you searching for?"

"Adam Reign."

"Give me a moment."

The minutes seemed to stretch toward eternity as the guard put me on hold. How long did it take to search for an inmate? Hours? Minutes? Days? Did the guard have a magical screen that would pop up whenever he needed valuable information such as that? Or would the guard simply say a name and a large book would open, pages flipping to the one that held that particular criminal's name?

My point was—weren't there about a thousand different magical means to quickly locate someone instead of me having to be on hold, sucking in air, not breathing, until the guard finally returned to the line and told me information that might or might not change my life?

"You're in luck," he said, suddenly sounding friendly. Perhaps he'd gotten a good talking to by his supervisor while I'd been on hold. Or perhaps it was almost time for him to go home. Probably that.

Or perhaps I was looking too deeply into things.

"What'd you find?" I asked, pressing the man, who was now whistling a tune into the phone. I guessed that also in prison people had all the time in the world. They might have in there, but I did not out here. I was aging while waiting for him to reveal the results of his search.

"Well," he replied, the sound of papers flipping in the background, "I had no problem finding the name that you gave me."

"Wonderful," I gushed. That could only mean one thing. Adam was safe and sou—

"The only problem was actually locating the inmate."

My shoulders sagged. "What do you mean, *locating him?* Isn't he there?"

"That's the thing. He's not."

My blood froze in my veins. Like, went solid as a chill spread from my head down through my chest and into my legs. "What do you mean, Adam Reign isn't there? Surely, you must be mistaken."

He was wrong. He would say that. In a moment the guard would chuckle fondly like I was a little girl and he was Santa Claus patting my head after I told him what I wanted for Christmas. Then the guard would say that I had misunderstood what he was trying to explain. Of course Adam Reign was there. He was absolutely there in that prison. He had misspoken. He'd given me misinformation.

"I'm not mistaken," he continued. I had been holding my breath so long that I started to get dizzy. I exhaled and made sure to let the air in and out in an attempt to keep myself from fainting. "Our records show that Adam Reign isn't here. He's gone. Has left the facility."

"But how is that possible? He was supposed to serve several years. Could you have picked up the wrong file? Do you need to talk to your supervisor?" I offered helpfully. No, I didn't like it when people asked to speak to my supervisor, of which those occasions had been few and far between, but this guy might've been asked that all the time. How did I know how things in prison worked?

"There's no mistake," he replied gruffly. I guessed he hadn't liked my supervisor reference after all. "Adam Reign is no longer in Witcheroo."

That could only mean one thing—Adam was here, in Magnolia Cove, pretending to be my husband.

CHAPTER 6

I could not alert the authorities. Sounded backward, didn't it? You would have thought my first act would be to find Sheriff Robb and tell him to arrest Adam.

But believe you me, that could have been a terrible mistake that would lead to devastating ends.

How did I know that? Because if Adam was pretending to be Axel, he was doing a darn fine job of it. He was doing such a good job, that even I couldn't tell them apart—and I was Axel's wife!

That meant I had to use other means to solve this problem. I would have to be smart. I would have to work smarter, not harder, as the saying went.

Though I did know lots of people who didn't mind working harder. I just didn't happen to be one of them. I like my vacations, if you know what I mean—especially ones that involve tropical settings and me drinking out of coconuts. I could even, on occasion, be persuaded to wear a coconut bra. Then again, that wasn't something that I'd done since giving birth. There might not be another coconut bra in my future. To be honest, I would be okay with that. It wasn't like coconut bras were the be-all-end-all of existence.

But anyway, back to the problem at hand.

What to do about Adam?

I needed a spell. That was what I had to do. I needed a spell that would reveal the truth of Adam's identity to me. The man wouldn't be cajoled into revealing himself. He also wouldn't be tricked. No. I would have to use magic.

The only problem (well, I supposed not the *only* one) was—how was he doing it? If Adam had been with me at dinner but Axel was at my shop cleaning up the mess, where had Axel gone?

Think, Pepper.

I had it! Nope, it didn't take me long to put myself in the shoes or brain of a criminal to figure out their evil plan.

This was what had occurred—after we left Ross's house, Axel had gone out to do some work. So he'd left me alone. When he returned home, it was well before dinner and he'd stayed at the house, not leaving until the next morning.

That person had been Adam.

Meanwhile, the real Axel had gone into town, done some work and fixed my store. He must've returned home later, but I'd been distracted cleaning up the kitchen and bathing Gizzy. Adam could have easily snuck out of the house, waited for Axel to arrive and then disposed of him all while I was giving the baby a bath.

But he wouldn't have wanted Axel dead. No, Axel would have information that Adam would need—stuff that could help Adam. So he would want Axel alive. Adam would want to hide his brother.

But where?

I had it. The one place where no one would look—the sewers.

Yes, that was totally how things had gone. So. I could search for Axel. Which might not have been such a terrible idea. I would find my husband, and then we would attack Adam together and get him sent back to prison where he belonged.

But I wouldn't send him to Witcheroo again. Clearly they couldn't keep up with their inmates. Heck, one had escaped right under their noses. That guard I'd spoken to didn't even seem all that concerned about it. Excuse me, but there were children in the world that needed protecting. The smallest thing that Witcheroo could do was make sure to keep violent criminals off the street—as was their job.

But first things first. I would deal with prison reform after finding Axel and arresting Adam.

All right. I had two options for plans—work the magic and find my husband. One had to be done first before I could do the other, but which one?

It made the most sense to locate Axel first. What if he was in danger? What if Adam was starving him in the sewers, and *why* was I so latched onto the idea of the sewers? Well, for one, there were magical places to hide a person, but people did on occasion visit the Conjuring Caverns. In my experience, no one ever said, *I've got a spell to work. Let's go down to the sewers and see how it goes.*

Nope. Didn't happen.

Which meant it was the perfect locale for hunting up my husband.

But first I had to make sure that everything was okay at home. After all, I couldn't let Adam think that I knew he was Adam. Also, I had to keep Gizzy safe, which meant that she would be spending less time at home and more time with Betty and Amelia. Luckily my daughter was still too young to understand a lot of grown-up talk, which meant that she wouldn't have to be subjected to Amelia's blathering on about all the colors of the rainbow that she had considered over the years for her wedding.

Not that I wasn't happy for my cousin. It was just that if you heard her reasoning once, you didn't need to relive the three-hour adventure again.

But I digressed.

I would call Betty first. She answered on the first ring. "Hello?"

Stunned by the sound clarity, I said, "Are you actually holding your phone the right way?"

"Yeah, Amelia showed me how."

"We've all shown you how."

"Sometimes it takes an old dog a few tries to learn a new trick."

Sometimes it took more than a few—like a hundred. "Well, you sound great. Listen, I've got a favor to ask. Can you watch Gizzy tonight?"

"No can do tonight. Shoo and me, we've got bingo at the old folks' home."

What? Since when? "But you don't even live in the old folks' home."

"Don't mean I can't play bingo," she said slyly, "and win."

"Don't you think that's like taking candy from a baby? Something you shouldn't do?"

"They have a sign that says, 'Everyone Welcome,'" she argued.

"Even worse. Aren't you worried they'll get you in there and then trap you? I can just see it," I explained. "The nursing home's ruse to get new patients is to trick people into going through their doors for an innocent game of bingo. Once you're inside, they lock the exits up tight and you're never allowed to leave."

"Shut your trap," Betty snarled. "There ain't nothing surreptitious going on over there. Just bingo. And it ain't even strip bingo."

Oh, Lawd. A visual that I did not need. "I thought there was only strip poker."

"Kid, you ain't lived long enough to know all the ins and outs of old folk life."

Sounded like I never wanted to know the ins and outs if strip bingo was involved. "So anyway. You can't watch Gizzy. Is that what you're saying?"

"That is what I'm saying. I think Amelia's got plans, too. But maybe Cordelia can. If she can't, why don't you just get Axel to watch her?"

"Er...he's got something going on." It was tempting to tell Betty the truth, it really was. But for this situation, I needed a delicate touch, and my grandmother's way to go about problems was much more bull-in-a-china-shop than anything else. If Adam got wind that we were on to him, then he'd react, possibly by taking Gizzy. There was no way that I was going to let him do that. But back to Betty. "I'll call Cordelia. Thanks."

I hung up with Betty and phoned my cousin, who was at work, preparing a wish for a girl about to turn sixteen. "She wants to fight in a battle and be the winner. She also wants to find love in the battle," my cousin explained. "Preferably by saving her man from getting impaled by a sword."

"I thought that love was against the rules of wishes," I said to Cordelia.

"It is, but *like* isn't. She can like a guy."

I frowned. "Would he even be real?"

"No. He'd be part of the wish. Not a real person, just imaginary, which is also part of the problem. She can't like shadow people. But anyway, that's something my dad and I are still working on. What's up?"

"Can you babysit for me tonight? There's something I've got to do."

"Sure. Larkin and I were just going to stay in, but I'm sure he wouldn't mind watching her."

Larkin was Cordelia's semi-new boyfriend and a fellow member of Axel's werewolf clan. "Isn't that a big step? Watching a baby together?"

"Um, yeah, I guess it is. But let's look at it this way—I can figure out what scares Larkin pretty quickly. If kids do, then I'll know that from the beginning. Besides, it's not as if I'm going to make him change a diaper. Wait. Maybe I should make him change *all* the diapers—really see if he sinks or swims."

I couldn't help but laugh. "You're truly evil, you know that?"

My cousin laughed maniacally. "A little poop never hurt anyone."

"No, I suppose not. Thanks. I owe you one."

"You're welcome."

We made plans for Cordelia to watch Gizzy at Betty's house, which meant that I wouldn't have to drop her off with my cousin, though I would pick her up once I'd located wherever Adam was hiding Axel in the sewers.

You think that I've jumped to conclusions, don't you? Well, to be honest, in that moment I was beginning to think so as well. After all, shlepping through dank water didn't sound like much fun and besides, there could have been a perfectly logical reason for how Axel could've been in two places at one time, and the guard I had spoken to earlier could've made a genuine mistake when it came to Adam's whereabouts.

All those thoughts were going through my head when I dialed Axel. Or Adam. Or Axel. I didn't know which one he was, and I was about to see if it was possible to find out.

It took a few rings before he picked up. Normally my husband was right on the phone, answering fast in case there was an emergency with Gizzy.

Not that we worried about my daughter, but you know how it was— new baby and all. Axel hadn't had much (any, really) experience with kids before we married, and he loved Gizzy with his whole heart. He adored her so much that when it came to her well-being, he worried. So he always answered my calls promptly in case something had happened.

Except for today. It took at least five rings before he picked up. "Hey, babe."

He never called me *babe*. "Hey, everything okay? You usually answer faster."

"Oh, yeah…I just couldn't get to the phone."

"The one in your pocket?"

"Um…I was engrossed in some research."

"Oh? What kind?"

It took him a second to answer. I didn't like that. "Someone's thinking of hiring me to help find a, uh, phoenix that disappeared."

"A phoenix? Since when did you become a monster hunter?"

"Since I got this call," he said with a laugh.

I tried to match his tone, but it felt like a pound of stones were grinding against one another in my gut. Axel took cases of missing people or things, husbands who needed to know if their wives were working magical spells behind their backs. He didn't search for magical beasts. In fact, he'd told me ages ago that he wouldn't take those sorts of cases because of the risks. Plenty of creatures were deadly. You couldn't predict how they would react, Axel had told me. That was why he'd never taken such a case before, because he always wanted to come home to me in one piece.

Was I supposed to think that he'd suddenly changed his mind? That he just happened to decide to go against rules that he had put into place?

Well no, I didn't believe that at all because I knew the truth. The man on the other line wasn't my husband. He was someone else entirely.

And I planned to prove it.

"Well," I said, "that sounds like fun research."

"It's not. It's boring."

Right. "Anyway, I was calling to let you know that I've got some extra work to do tonight. Oh, and thank you, by the way, for fixing my shop windows."

He hesitated. "You're welcome."

"But anyway, I'll be out late and Cordelia said she'd watch Gizzy, so don't wait on us for supper. We'll already be fed."

"I don't mind watching Gizzy," he told me.

"Over my dea—oh, sure. I know. But this is easier." I didn't want to slip up again like I just nearly had. "Listen, I'll call you later, okay?"

"Okay. Love you," he said before hanging up.

I pretended not to hear him as I thumbed the red button on my phone, ending the call.

CHAPTER 7

How to hunt for the man you love: The first thing you did was make sure that nobody knew your true love was missing. Well, I'd already done that.

The second thing was to be sure to pick the scariest place on earth to search.

Y'all, the sewers were dark and smelled like the inside of someone's intestines. I wasn't joking. One time, when I was at my grandparent's farm when I was little, my grandpa had shot a deer and was gutting it. Well, his knife missed and he wound up nicking the intestines. Boy, had they stunk. The stench was so vile that I nearly puked.

Come to think of it, I *had* puked.

So that was what the sewers smelled like. In order to deal with the stench, I magicked up a nose bubble and placed it on my face, where it snuggly attached to my skin.

Once the smell part was under control, the next thing I did was focus on light. I rubbed my hands together, and as they warmed, a stick formed between them. With a spark of power, a flame ignited on one end, and that became my torch of light.

I stepped slowly at first, making sure the water didn't seep into the rain boots I'd had the forethought to swap my fashion boots for. The dank liquid didn't seem to penetrate the thick rubber, which was a relief. If the stench of the water got on my skin, I had the feeling that I'd have a heck of a time getting it off. It might be worse than trying to rub skunk out of you—and that required bathing in tomato sauce. There was no telling what I'd have to swim in to get the smell of poop off me.

And to be honest, I didn't want to have to think about it.

Even with all that—the boots, the nose covering, and the torch, there was still no mistaking the fact that I was in a sewer by myself searching for Axel.

The air inside the tunnel was cool and moist. Humidity clung to my skin, making my flesh crawl. A rat scurried toward me, and I jumped as it raced under my feet. I gripped the side of the tunnel as my heart pounded.

Get ahold of yourself, Pepper.

I could not be jumping at every small thing. This was a sewer. It would be filled with creatures small and...small. There would be rats, probably mice. There might even be a lizard or two. Seeing them run past was a small price to pay for saving my husband—who'd better be down here, by the way. I was going to a lot of trouble to get him back.

As I walked the tunnels, I came to a split in the path. Suddenly my bright idea didn't seem so smart anymore. How big was the sewer system? Magnolia Cove wasn't that large of a town. Betty's house was on the sewer system, but only about half a mile away, those folks were on septic. So the tunnels couldn't run that far. Perhaps it would have been best if I simply called out for Axel.

But what if he couldn't hear me? Or worse, what if he couldn't respond? Adam wouldn't just leave him in the sewer to run around and escape. He would have immobilized his brother. Oh, how I disliked Adam the more I thought of what he'd done. That guy was going to pay for the suffering he had inflicted on my family.

Seriously.

But back to the split in the tunnels. I didn't know which way to go, had not one clue. I also didn't have a map of the system on me, which I suddenly realized hadn't been very smart. Before I'd come down, I should've contacted public works and gotten one. Or at least "borrowed" one from them. Because you knew how that conversation would've gone. I would've asked politely for a map. The supervisor would've asked why I needed it. Not wanting to tell the truth, I would've made up a lie like, something fell in, or I'm doing research on the history of Magnolia Cove's sewers to present to a kindergarten class. Then the supervisor would've been so intrigued by my presentation he probably would've given me a tour of the tunnels himself, which would have ruined my entire plan.

Yes, it was better that I was going blindly into this thing. That way I could walk wherever I wanted. Speaking of, I was still standing at the fork.

"Okay, to the right will lead me closer to the center of town." At least I thought so. "The left will lead me away."

Since Axel had helped place Adam in prison, Adam would want some sort of revenge. Farther away from town, there wouldn't be as much action. But closer to the center, there would be more water spilling in from rain, more garbage and probably more rats.

So to the center of town, I went.

It would have been great to say that the sewer became less creepy, but that would have been an utter lie. In fact, more water leaked down the walls the farther I went. But my hopes rose because I felt like I was on the right track.

Boy, Axel would be relieved to see me when I found him. I would win wife of the year or something. I couldn't wait to see the expression of happiness on his face. He'd be so impressed, wondering how I figured out that he'd been captured to begin with.

That was what I focused on as I picked my way through the near darkness. The torch didn't light the tunnel too far ahead, which meant I had to walk slowly, making sure that I didn't step on any rats that were hiding exactly where my foot was about to land.

Even though I knew that I was on to something, I was starting to doubt my brilliant plan. The tunnels were eerily empty, and the only signs of life were the occasional rodent. As I reached another fork in the road, a flash of movement caught my attention. I pitched the torch forward to see, and a streak of white caught my attention.

"What in the world?" I whispered.

Then a sound, one that I hadn't expected to hear, rang in my ears.

"*Mewww.*"

A kitten! The sound was a kitten. "Hello?"

The little ball of white fur darted away at my voice, but then paused as if deciding what to do next. Then little white legs scampered toward me, and the kitten stepped into the torchlight.

"You," I said, gasping.

The kitten sniffed my leg, immediately broke out into a purr and rubbed its body against my shin. *Preggers!*

I rolled my eyes at the ridiculous nickname that the puppies and kittens had given me when I was pregnant. Even though this kitten hadn't been around while I was carrying Gizzy, the nickname had unfortunately been passed down from one kitten to the next and didn't look like it was going to be extinguished anytime soon.

Though the name annoyed me, seeing the kitten filled me with hope. I scooped her up and pressed her to my chest. "What are you doing down here? How did you get here?"

She answered telepathically. *We all came.*

My heart skidded to a stop. "What do you mean, 'we all came'?"

After the boom, she replied.

The boom. She must have been referring to the explosion of glass from the windows and doors. This was worse than I thought. Of course! Adam had gone to Familiar Place when he first arrived in town. Still ticked at me for having played a part in his incarceration, the man had destroyed my shop and released all my animals in revenge.

It made perfect sense.

"Where are the others?" I asked the kitten.

I lost them. I don't know.

"Then we'll find them." I magicked up a sling that crossed over my shoulder, and tucked the kitten into it. "Stay in there no matter what happens. I'll keep you safe."

Within seconds I felt the vibration of her purr. It hurt my heart that she and the other animals had been so traumatized. If Adam had a problem, then he should have faced off against me about it. There had been no reason to involve my poor animals. They were innocents in all this.

Yep. He would pay.

The kitten seemed to fall asleep after a few minutes, and I kept my eyes and ears open in case I came across another creature. The way she talked, it seemed like others should have been in the tunnels somewhere. Surely I'd come across them if I just traveled far enough.

I came to yet another split and was about to go right when a scratching sound came from the left.

Was it one of my animals? Was it Axel?

My heart thundered as I turned in the direction of the noise. The torch beam had weakened over the course of my walk. Apparently it had used up a lot of the fuel that I had started with. That told you how long I'd been down there. When magical fuel weakened, you knew it had been running a while.

The reason why that was important to know is because I'd only stepped a few feet when I swore that a shadow loomed ahead of me. It was hard to distinguish because of the weakened light and all. So I thrust the torch forward.

"Axel?" I whispered.

What sounded like snoring came from the belly of the sewers. If it was snoring, I thought, then surely I had reached Axel. I'd found him.

My heart leaped with joy. I approached slowly, not wanting to startle him. How he could have been sleeping in the sewer, I didn't know. But it wasn't my place to judge. It was my place to save him.

And be considered wife of the year.

Just kidding.

Sort of.

But as I neared, I noticed that the shadow didn't seem quite right. It was long, very long, dark and almost scaly. Axel didn't have scales. Not even when he was a werewolf. Then, he had silky fur that covered him from head to toe.

I flicked my hand at the torch, and the light flared bright and hot, allowing me to see better.

The form before me did indeed have scales. It was also dark green and long, with a thick, corrugated tail.

I sucked air, shocked at the image that poured into my eyes, and unable to comprehend exactly what it was. You know, when your brain sees a picture that is so unbelievable, you can't quite, well, *believe* what you're witnessing.

That was how that moment was.

The creature's head swung dramatically in my direction. Yellow eyes glared at me, and huge jaws opened, releasing a growl that made the tunnel vibrate.

A jolt of fear raced down to my toes as I realized that I had come face-to-face with—an alligator!

CHAPTER 8

What in the world was an alligator doing in the tunnels? Why was there an alligator in front of me? How had it gotten down here?

In that moment I swore that someone had pulled me out of Magnolia Cove and dropped me into a bad eighties movie where an alligator who lived in the sewers was terrorizing an entire city.

Right, I remembered thinking, *as if that could happen.*

Well, it was happening! In fact, coming toward me was an alligator, its jaws open as if it was ready to eat me.

My brain suddenly cracked in two. I am not even joking.

I couldn't put two coherent thoughts together. All I could come up with was: I had come here to find Axel. Now there was a beast looking like it wanted to eat me (which it probably did). Had the gator eaten Axel?

What in the world was happening?

Lucky for me, my brain decided to wake up from the fog covering it and jump into action.

So I turned and ran.

Unfortunately the alligator started running, too.

I still carried the torch, so I sneaked a peek behind me as I barreled through the tunnels. Alligators couldn't run quickly on land. I'd learned that when I was like ten, from watching *Nature* on PBS. Oh, they were swifter than a boat in water, but get a gator on land and they couldn't keep up with their prey. They were cumbersome, their log bodies hard to maneuver.

Needless to say, I was super confident that when I peered over my shoulder, I was not going to see said gator.

But I was wrong.

The beast was keeping up with me, its legs pumping swiftly. I had to speed up, keep going, outrun the creature before I became its next meal.

My brain screamed at me to move faster, to go as quickly as I could, and my muscles complied. Already my thighs were bunching up; my quadriceps were knotting. When was the last time I had worked out? I couldn't even remember. That was it—as soon as tomorrow hit, I would be out, running, getting my body back into shape. I would cut out the jelly beans and only eat chicken and steamed broccoli.

Who was I kidding? I couldn't give up jelly beans.

Behind me, the creature roared. A jolt of panic raced down my spine. It was right behind me. It was catching up.

Think, Pepper.

Okay, so this was a magical alligator and it could run as fast as a person. There was no way that I could outrun it for long. So I had to do something different.

I had to use magic.

It couldn't climb, which meant it was stuck in the tunnels. But I could do better than that. I could escape with just a though—

And suddenly I was out of the sewer and standing aboveground in the middle of Bubbling Cauldron Road. Like, right in the middle.

I exhaled a deep breath and bent over, gripping my knees. Air entered my lungs in thick gulps, which did nothing to settle my heart. It jackhammered against my chest, threatening to pop out onto the asphalt.

It took several long moments before my body began to settle down. My brain was on a roller coaster. It was impossible for me to believe what I'd seen, but there was no doubt in my mind as to the truth of it.

There was an alligator living in the sewers of Magnolia Cove. Why? How? I didn't even want to think that the creature had harmed my husband. But what if it had?

"Hello? Are you all right?"

I picked my head up and spotted a woman walking hesitantly toward me. She had long dark hair that was plaited into two ropes of braids that cascaded over each shoulder. She was young, early twenties most likely, with a worried expression creasing her brow.

"Do you understand me?" she asked.

Boy, I must've looked bad if the woman thought I couldn't speak. I swallowed a few times, wetting my parched mouth. "Yes, I understand you, and no, I'm not okay."

Her worried expression deepened. "Do you want me to call someone for you? Can I get someone?" When I didn't answer, she added, "My name's Ellen."

Ellen? Where had I heard that name before? "You're Ross's wife?"

She blinked in surprise. "Yes. How do you know Ross?"

"We went there, to your house, my husband and me, searching for my lost animals."

Her eyes widened. "You're Pepper?"

"Yes."

Of course none of the pleasantries of meeting seemed important as there was an alligator on the loose. That needed to be dealt with first. We needed to get the beast out of there, and quickly.

Ellen moved closer, her hands reaching to comfort me. "Pepper, you don't look good. Maybe I should get you home."

"No. I just came from the sewers."

Her nose wrinkled. I wasn't sure if that was because I smelled or because she thought it was disgusting that I'd been sewer diving. You know, like dumpster diving, except being in a sewer. I wondered if that could have been called *sewer spelunking*, if that could become a trend. Perhaps I would work on it.

Then again, there were a lot of other things to focus on, so perhaps sewer spelunking would get put on the back burner where it belonged.

"What were you doing in the sewer?" she asked.

"Looking for my..." If I told her that I was looking for Axel, then others might find out about Adam. I couldn't simply have Adam arrested, because then he wouldn't tell me what he'd done with my husband. I had to be smart about this. "I was looking for...my animals. They got lost a few days ago. But I saw something else—an alligator."

She frowned for a moment, but then said, "Ross told me about your animals." Ellen wasn't at all disturbed by me mentioning an alligator. She probably thought I'd imagined it. "Is that why you were in the sewer? Looking for them?"

"I found her," I told her, presenting the kitten. The creature in the sling yawned and stretched, totally oblivious to the fact that we'd narrowly escaped certain death. "See?"

Ellen's gaze trailed down the creature strapped to my chest. "Oh. Well...you found that down there?"

I nodded. "And I think there are more." If they'd managed to escape the gator's clutches, that was. "I just have to find them."

She placed her arms around me. "You don't need to be looking for anything tonight. Right now, it seems as if you could use a shower and a warm bed."

I glanced down at my clothes, which were splattered with mud and goodness knew what else. As much as I wanted to return to the tunnels, Ellen was right. The best thing for me in that moment was to get some rest, eat and regroup, come up with a plan for the next day.

I pushed my shoulders back and lifted my chin. "You know, Ellen, I think you're right."

She smiled warmly at me. "Let me get you wherever it is you need to go. Come on. I'll walk with you."

I let her lead me off, and for some reason it didn't occur to me to ask Ellen what she was doing out on Bubbling Cauldron all alone. My brain was too scrambled to think clearly, as I'd mentioned.

But I wished that I had asked her because it would've saved a lot of turmoil—the sort that could destroy everything.

CHAPTER 9

There was a little problem about what to do next. So I'd discovered an alligator in the sewer. I'd also located one of my animals in the underbelly of Magnolia Cove. Plus, I was convinced that my husband wasn't my husband.

All those things meant that I had to come up with a plan, and fast.

The first thing to do was get Gizzy from Cordelia and Larkin. The baby was asleep when I arrived at Betty's. The television was on and my cousin and her boyfriend were watching a show where celebrity witches put glamours on themselves and then sang songs. The judges had to guess who the famous singers were on their voice alone.

But I digress. As soon as I stepped through the door, Cordelia's eyes widened. Oops. I'd forgotten to clean myself up a bit after having been sloshing around in the sewer.

"You okay?" she asked.

"Me? I'm fine." I waved away her concern. "I'm all good."

Larkin was Axel's cousin, and if truth be told, he had a bit of the Reign look and appeal. His rust-colored hair was thick and wavy, and his eyes were piercing, fierce like my husband's. It wasn't hard to see why Cordelia was attracted to him.

Larkin raked his fingers through his hair and shot Cordelia an uncomfortable glance. "Looks like it's getting late. I'd best be going. Got to make sure all the werewolves are locked up tight."

He didn't, actually, have to make sure of that because his fellow clan members were perfectly capable of locking themselves up if they needed to. But I appreciated Larkin's attempt at an excuse to leave, seeing as how I was a mess and all.

Cordelia kissed his cheek. "Good night."

"Night." He gave my shoulder a squeeze. "Nice to see you, and Gizzy was easy tonight. She didn't cry once."

"Great," I replied with a smile. "Thanks for watching her."

"Anytime."

He shot Cordelia a smile and then exited the house. As soon as he was gone, the grin on my cousin's face melted.

"What in the world happened to you?"

I shrugged. "Me? I just fell while I was walking here from the store. No big deal."

"You're lying."

I scoffed. "I have no idea what you're talking about."

"Yes, you do. Because you're fibbing." She pulled her long blonde hair over one shoulder and twisted it like she was trying to wring water from it. "I know that I don't care about things. Or at least I don't let on that I do. My general disposition is sarcastic and sour. I get that. But I'd be lying if I said that I didn't care about you and that concern has me worried."

"I don't know why."

She gestured upstairs. "Because you have a baby and a husband and you're off galivanting, obviously up to things that Axel doesn't know about, because otherwise why would you be a mess?"

Not interested in getting into this conversation, I headed toward the stairs. "Is Gizzy up here?"

"Yes, but you're not getting her. Not until you tell me what's going on."

I laughed, unsure if the sound seemed convincing. "Nothing's going on. Now, if you don't mind, I'm going to get my daughter." I started up the stairs as Cordelia threw up her hand. Next thing I knew, I'd walked smack into a force field. It took everything I had to tamp down my anger. Even still, my next words came grinding out. "What are you doing?"

"Making you talk to me because you're obviously up to something. Is this about your animals?"

Seeing an easy way out, I crossed to the couch and slumped down on it. "Yes, it's about the animals." I pulled the kitten from the sling. Cordelia sat beside me, and I handed the fuzzball to her. The kitten was still sleeping and barely stirred as she was palmed into a warm hand. "I found her tonight."

"Where?"

To tell or not to tell, that was the question. "In the sewers," I admitted. I mean, what was I keeping it a secret for? I had to find Axel, and the alligator obviously had to be dealt with, otherwise someone or some people could get hurt. I have mentioned that I saw that movie where the gator terrorized an entire city, right? I couldn't let that happen to Magnolia Cove.

But Cordelia did not take my mention of the tunnels of sludge that burrowed beneath our town very well—or, at least as well as I'd hoped she might.

"The sewers?" she shouted, recoiling from me. "What were you doing there?"

I waved away her concern. "Oh, nothing."

"Pepper," she warned, "if you don't tell me, I'll tell Axel."

My eyes flared. "No, don't do that."

"Why not?" she asked as she stroked the kitten.

I sighed. Here went nothing. "Because I'm worried that Axel isn't Axel."

She laughed. "What are you talking about?"

"I know for a fact that he was in two places at once, and then I called the prison to make sure that Adam, his twin, was still incarcerated, and guess what? They couldn't find him."

"So you think—wait, let me wrap my brain around this." Cordelia closed her eyes; her long lashes brushed her cheeks. When she opened them, she exhaled very slowly. "You believe that your husband isn't your husband, is that it?"

"How else can you explain the fact that he was one place when I know for a fact that he was in another? That's blood magic, if you work it with a spell. And no one would have glamoured themself to be him. Plus, it makes sense. Who else would've destroyed my shop? Adam hates me, I'm sure. He would want to exact his revenge."

She grimaced. "I'm still trying to wrap my head around this. So you think...what, exactly?"

"That Adam took over Axel's life. That I'm living with Adam and that Axel is tied up in the sewers."

It sounded ridiculous when I said it like that, but earlier it had made a lot more sense to me.

Cordelia covered her face with her free hand. "You went down in the sewers because you think that's where Axel is?"

"It seems like a good place for Adam to stash him."

She thought about that a moment. "But why the sewer? Why not someplace else?"

Did I have to explain everything? "Because no one goes down there. If he put him anywhere else, Adam would risk Axel being found and his plan uncovered."

"What exactly is his plan?"

"Take over his life? Destroy the clan, his family?"

"Hmmm."

"You're not convinced."

She shook her head. "No, it's not that. It's not that I'm not convinced. It's that...maybe you need a vacation." My cousin smiled tightly. "You've had a lot going on with the baby and work, and then someone let all your animals go or stole them. Well, you found one kitten, so maybe they didn't steal them."

"She told me that they had been all together and she got separated," I said with confidence. There. That would prove I wasn't cracking up. "You could ask her, but you don't speak cat."

Cordelia glanced at the kitten warmly. "Yes, that would be a problem, because I don't. But what I'm saying is, maybe you need to take some time off."

"You don't believe me," I said flatly. "This was why I shouldn't have told you. I completely forgot how ridiculous I looked; otherwise I would've cleaned up before I walked in." I dropped my head into my hands in frustration. "Cordelia, I know this sounds crazy. I know it seems completely unbelievable. But you have to trust me—something is going on. Axel would never work dark magic like that. He just wouldn't. There would be no reason for him to. And the person who saw him was Harry from Castin' Iron. He might be old and a little crazy, but he knows my husband."

She sighed. "Why don't you just ask him?"

"Because Adam is gone! He's not in the prison. What do you want me to ask?"

She raised her voice to match mine. "So you go traipsing into the sewer? Amelia's getting married soon. You're married. You've got a family. Don't you think that for once, you should be thinking of other people and not yourself?"

Her words bit into my skin like a sword. I stared at my cousin, unable to believe that she would have said such a thing to me. I wasn't doing any of this because I was being selfish. I was trying to save my husband; couldn't she see that? But somehow my actions had been flipped on me, and I was trudging through sewer tunnels in order to bring attention to myself. That was how she saw this. That was how she saw me—as a spoiled, selfish woman.

Tears brimmed in my eyes, but I refused to blink and let them spill onto my cheeks. "I didn't realize that you felt that way."

Her expression fell. "Pepper, I'm sorry. Look. That didn't come out right. All I'm saying is, we've found ourselves in some crazy situations before, but are you even listening to yourself? You're saying that your husband isn't your husband, but instead of talking to him or asking him about what you know, you head dive into the sewers to prove that your hypothesis is right. The *sewers*, Pepper. Does that even make sense? It's the last place that Axel would be. If Adam wanted to hurt Axel, why wouldn't he simply show up and fight him with magic? Why would he then stow your husband below us? It makes no sense. Don't you see that?"

She was right. When it was put that way, none of it made sense. I had to agree with her. It was an insane, crazy plan. But for some reason I simply couldn't let it go. There was something going on with Axel. My gut told me so.

But perhaps the best way to deal with Cordelia was to pretend that everything was hunky-dory. Just go with the flow.

So I smiled and nodded. "You're right. I should focus on other things."

"Pepper," she said with defeat, "don't be like that. I know you're only saying that because you think it's what I want to hear."

"No." I did my best to sound more genuine. "Not at all. You're right. My plan was insane. It was ridiculous. Foolish. Why I ever thought Axel would be tied up in the sewers is beyond me. No rational person would think that way. I guess everything that happened with Familiar Place has simply been too much. It's all been a strain. I see that now. It took me coming here for you to convince me."

Cordelia rubbed my arm. "Look, if you want to leave Gizzy here tonight, I'd understand. Betty won't care, either. I'm sure of it."

Perhaps that would have been best. After all, I didn't want to take her home to that imposter. "Thank you. Sounds like a wonderful idea. I could use the rest."

"That's what I was thinking." She smiled and rose. "Just get some sleep, okay? See how you feel in the morning. We can talk about it then."

"Yes, let's do that."

Cordelia handed the kitten back to me. "You want her?"

Mattie wasn't always great with other cats. She liked Mr. Jingles okay. But a kitten? I wasn't sure how she would react. "No, keep her here until tomorrow. I'll get her then."

"Great." Cordelia guided me to the center of the room. "I'll whisk you back to your house."

"Thank you. I definitely don't want to return to the sewers tonight."

She opened a portal. "Oh? Too gross?"

"Nope." I took a step toward the magic swirling in the room. "I barely escaped the alligator that's living there." The portal began to close around me as Cordelia's jaw dropped in astonishment. "If I go back, I might wind up its dinner."

She gaped at me as the portal closed.

CHAPTER 10

"What do you mean, there's an alligator in the sewers?"

First thing the next morning, Betty showed up at my front door. I supposed that was thanks to Cordelia, who had decided to believe me about something—namely, the gator creeping around in the tunnels beneath our feet.

Adam was in the kitchen, whistling and washing up a juice glass that he'd just drank out of, when my grandmother appeared. He tossed a dish towel over one shoulder and crossed to the open door, where I stood, face burning.

I'd only said that to Cordelia to shut her up about me having gone crazy. I hadn't expected her to tell the entire world.

"Well?" Betty demanded of me. "You told your cousin about a creature. Is it true?"

I glanced over at Axel or Adam or whoever he was. He lifted his brows in question. "I don't know anything about it," he said.

He *would* say that. When I'd gotten in the night before, he'd already been asleep, so I couldn't watch him for tells that he wasn't my husband. He'd been concerned when he woke up, asking about Gizzy, which I'd quickly smoothed over by saying she was sleeping so soundly that I hadn't wanted to wake her at Betty's. After that, he acted ridiculously normal, like too normal, as if Adam wanted to throw me off the scent.

Which had only worked out to confuse me more, if you wanted to know the truth. If Adam was pretending to be Axel, he was being a very, very calm and normal Axel—almost too calm and normal, know what I mean?

But anyway, now Betty knew about the alligator and so did Adam. Yes, I was going to call him Adam because I wasn't convinced that he wasn't.

I sagged against the edge of the door. "Yes, there's an alligator in the sewers. Saw it last night."

"The sewers?" Adam asked. "How would you even know that?"

I scrambled to come up with an answer. "I was looking for the animals from my shop and got a wild hair that they could be down there."

"What would ever give you that wild hair?" he growled.

"We've searched everywhere else," I snapped. "It seemed like a good idea."

"Well, stay out of there," he commanded.

Oh, now he'd done it. I would *not* stay out of there now. "Why? Why's it so important that I don't go there?"

He lifted his hands in disbelief. "Do I really have to explain that those places could be dangerous? For goodness' sake, you just saw an alligator."

I lifted my brows in question. "Is that really why you don't want me snooping in the sewers?" Or was it because he was hiding my husband down there?

"Yes," he snarled. "Isn't that reason enough?" To Betty he said, "Come on in. I'll make coffee while *my wife* tells us exactly what happened."

I watched every movement Adam made while he brewed the drink. Unfortunately he did it to perfection. There was no catching him stumbling with his magic when he brewed the dark liquid.

It was so annoying, y'all.

But anyway, if I thought that I was going to get any sympathy from Betty, I was wrong. Soon as she had a cup of Joe in hand, she laid into me.

"According to Cordelia, you had some harebrained plan, which she didn't go into, by the way."

I exhaled with relief.

Betty continued. "You went down into the sewers, found a kitten and then was chased by a gator."

I clapped my hands. "Seems like I don't need to explain anything. You've got the whole story, every bit of it. That's exactly what happened."

Betty's eyes narrowed. "And you were down there searching for your animals," she said in a really accusing voice, which caught me off guard.

"Yes," I replied slowly, unsure if that was the right or wrong answer. "I was."

"Hmmm. Are you sure that was the only reason you were down there?"

"Why is everyone so worried about me going down into the sewers? What's the big deal?"

"Nothing," she said quickly, too quickly.

I shot Adam a concerned look before I remembered who he was. He shot me the same look. That irked me.

"Betty," I said in my most warning voice, "what's down there? What's in the sewers?"

"Nothing, not one thing." She rose quickly. "Thank you for the coffee. But I believe that I must be going."

I magicked myself to the door, blocking her path to escape. Yes, she could still have used magic, but this was very dramatic and worked. Her eyes widened in fear.

Fear, I tell you.

"What's in the sewer that you're so worried about?" I asked again.

She gave Adam a look that said, *Help me*, but he just furrowed his brow. "Pepper's right. You're hiding something. What is it, Betty?"

Realizing that she wasn't going to receive any help from my husband, Betty crossed her arms. "For the last time, nothing's wrong. But seeing as how there's an alligator in our sewers, I would say it's time to call the sheriff and have him deal with it."

As much as I didn't want to bring any more attention to the whole Axel/Adam thing, I was relieved. If we went down to the sewers and

Mullins Rob saw Axel, he'd have no choice but to believe my story. Getting the law involved could help me more than I realized.

I sneaked a glance at Adam, but his expression was blank. *Great.* His poker face was unreadable. But that didn't matter. Now we had a next step, a good one at that.

Smiling, I said, "Good idea. Let's call Mullins Rob."

~

Downtown was a mess. As soon as Mullins Rob was contacted, he gathered every last wizard and witch police officer and stationed them smack in the middle of Bubbling Cauldron Road.

A huge swath of the street was cordoned off, which was causing congestion for the small amount of traffic that we had. Yellow police tape was strung from one side of the road to the other, and it formed a square that happened to hold, in its very center, one sewer cap.

It was probably dumb to mention to Mullins Rob that there were dozens of sewer entries in town. Anyone could go in at one of those points. But when Betty had told him that the sewer downtown held an alligator, apparently he had taken her quite literally.

"Pepper. Axel," he said as he greeted us.

I couldn't help but flinch at my husband's name being worn by the imposter beside me. Adam shook the sheriff's hand in one of those manly bonding sorts of ways. "We came as quickly as we could," he said.

Betty shoved up her sleeves. "What'cha got? Anything yet?"

"We were waiting for you." The sheriff's dark gaze landed on me, and a shiver zinged down my spine. "Pepper, you're sure there's an alligator down there? I've got all my men here, ready to tackle the creature."

I nodded. "I'm positive. Saw it last night."

Mullins squinted his one eye. "Then we'll go in and search."

I balled up my fists. "Great. Where are we going?"

He laughed. "You're not coming with us."

The insult made my cheeks burn. "Of course I am. I know where you can find it."

"We have enough men to search all the tunnels. I won't have a civilian getting hurt," he told me.

"So you'd rather your men go in blind," I argued.

Betty hoisted herself between us, boobs leading the way. "I'm afraid that my granddaughter's right. We're going down with y'all."

Now it was Mullins's turn for his cheeks to redden. "I won't have a bunch of civilians—"

"Who are you calling civilians?" Betty demanded. "I've lived in this town for practically forever. My granddaughter saw that alligator last night. She can lead the way. And just to make sure that the integrity of our town remains as such, I'm tagging along."

"For goodness' sake," Mullins Rob.

"You can call goodness all you want," Betty quipped. "It won't change anything. We're going, whether you like it or not."

The sheriff shot Adam a pleading look. "Isn't there anything you can do to talk them out of this?"

The sheriff had not yet learned that once Betty Craple got an idea in her head, there was no convincing her otherwise. Betty was the sort that if something came to her—an idea for a recipe or even a plan, nothing, not one thing would get in her way until that plan was executed.

Not even the law.

As y'all could probably tell, there was the same blood in me.

But anyway, Mullins was giving Adam pleading looks, and all my faux husband did was shrug. "Betty has her reasons. If the sewers must remain intact in order to keep our town safe, then so be it."

Mullins shook his head in disgust. "We're not going to destroy the tunnels," he told Betty.

"Good." She brushed past him and added over her shoulder, "I can't wait to make sure that's true."

Mullins's face was red as a maraschino cherry, my least favorite type to eat. I just didn't get it. Cherries were amazing fresh. Why can them at all? But I digressed.

The sheriff turned to his men, lifted his finger and swirled it around. "Come on, boys. We're going in—with company."

If Mullins's deputies were ticked that we were there, they didn't let on. They silently led the way through the tunnels, lights on, searching for the beast that inhabited the sewer.

Adam was in the lead with Mullins, for our protection, he had told me. Right. He wanted to make sure that we didn't find anything that we weren't supposed to. For all I knew, he had set the alligator loose himself to keep guard over Axel in order to make sure that no one found him.

My gut was telling me that Adam would do whatever he could to keep us far, far away from the creature. Which meant that I had to be on high alert.

Betty walked beside me, both of us bringing up the rear. Alligators were creatures of habit, according to Mullins Rob, who had done a little bit of preliminary research before stepping foot underground. He'd said that the beast would keep to its same hunting ground. All I had to do was direct them toward it.

We came to a fork in the path. "Which way?" Mullins asked from the front of the line.

"Right," I told him.

The men splintered off to the right. I started to follow, but Betty hesitated. "Go on," she said. "After you."

Not thinking too much about it, because I had no reason to believe that my grandmother would be deceptive in any way, I followed the men to the right.

But when I looked behind me, Betty had taken the path in the opposite direction. *Great*. What was she up to? And was she trying to get herself killed? Did she want to face off against the alligator herself, prove that she was some sort of geriatric monster hunter?

But as I watched her skulking off, it occurred to me that she didn't appear to be searching for the gator. Her shoulders weren't pinched back, her arms weren't up and ready. Instead Betty was moving as if she were hiding, as if she didn't want to be noticed.

Which of course meant that I would have to go after her and find out exactly what was going on.

I slipped away from the rest of the crew and sidled up to my grandmother. "Just what do you think you're doing?"

She jolted before scowling at me. "You could give an old lady a heart attack, sneaking up on me like that."

"A heart attack? You're going to live forever. You and I both know it."

"It is in my plan," she said slyly. "But what are you messing about on? Get back to the others."

"Only if you come with me."

Her silence told me everything. She wasn't going back. Betty was on her own mission. But what was that? Perhaps she was on the exact mission that I was, that she knew about Adam but hadn't told me about it because she was afraid that I wouldn't believe her.

Betty said nothing, only continued walking. It would be best if we were on the same page, I thought, so I said, "It's okay if you don't want to tell me. I already know what's going on."

She came to a halt and took my shoulders, staring into my eyes, searching for something. "You know? And you didn't say anything?"

"Of course not. We can't have him finding out."

She sighed with relief. "Not at all. If he knew, he'd be searching down here himself."

"But he already is," I told her.

She released me and rubbed her chin. "It's unfortunate but can't be helped. If he knew about it, he'd be wanting to dig it up."

"Right, because he's— Wait a minute. What are you talking about?"

My grandmother scowled. "What's buried. What are you talking about?"

"Adam."

"Who?"

"Um. Never mind. What do you mean, what's buried?"

She shook her head. "Come on. I'll show you. You've come this far anyway; you might as well know about it."

I would have been lying to say that curiosity had not gotten ahold of me. What was so important to Betty down here? Why be so secretive?

A thousand questions pelted my mind, and it took all my restraint not to shoot them at my grandmother. But I had known her long enough to realize that everything would be revealed in its own good time.

We took two more rights and walked. We must've been close to her neighborhood by that time. The voices of the sheriff and his posse had long since quieted, leaving Betty and me alone, the only sound the sloshing of our feet and the occasional rat scurrying by.

It would've been great luck if we just so happened to come across more of the animals from my store. But if truth be told, I would rather have found my husband than a kitten or puppy.

After a little ways we took one last left and came to a dead end. The tunnel actually stopped, blocked by bricks. Betty laid a hand on it and sighed. "Thank goodness."

"What's that?"

It took her a long moment before she answered. "What lies buried here is something we put away a long time ago. Something that nearly destroyed the witches and wizards. If it ever got out again, we'd be done for."

CHAPTER 11

"Whoa. What are you talking about? There's an evil entity living right below our feet? How long has it been here, and were you ever going to tell me?"

"No," she said sharply.

I flinched. Betty could be a lot of things, secretive for sure. But she genuinely shared information. But this? It was difficult to wrap my head around because she was usually very giving. But the fact that this secret was one she was willing to take to her grave unsettled me.

"Why won't you tell me?" I ventured, knowing that nothing would have been gained by just sitting back and waiting for her to decide if she was going to tell me what this was all about.

"Because some things are best unknown." The hand resting on the brick slid down to her side. My grandmother nodded as if satisfied that everything was in its place—every stone sturdy, every inch of mortar secure. "But since you're here, I might as well tell you."

"Please do."

"A long time ago—well, before you were born, anyway, when your mother was still with us—a witch moved into Magnolia Cove. She seemed nice enough, befriending all of us. And we, in kind, were nice to her, making blueberry bread and other treats in greeting."

"You've never made me blueberry bread."

She frowned. "That is neither here nor there."

"It's kind of here, since you mentioned it."

Betty rolled her eyes. "Fine. I will make you some."

"Thank you."

"Now, may I continue?" When I nodded, she went on. "The witch became part of our community like anyone else. But what we didn't know was that she had dark intentions."

"Don't they all?" I murmured.

Betty shot me a quick look before continuing. "She had arrived in our town not to be our friend, but to ferret out our secrets and to steal from us, which she did. The witch broke into the Vault to claim one of the worst curses that I know of."

"What was it?" I asked.

But she ignored me. "We almost didn't catch her in time before she left. But whenever a person breaks into the Vault, there is nothing quiet about it. We were quickly alerted to her presence, and we caught up to her, forcing the witch to hand over the curse. But she didn't. Instead she unleashed it on all of us, spraying the town with magic."

My stomach knotted. "What did it do? Did it turn you all into bats? Condemn your ground so that you'd never grow anything again?"

"Worse," Betty said coldly.

What could have been worse than being transformed? Oh, I knew what. "Did it take all the love from the world?"

That would have been worse. A world without love was no world that I wanted to live in.

But Betty shook her head. "No. It made all of us happy."

Had I heard her correctly? "I'm sorry. It did what?"

"Gave us unbounding joy."

Was she kidding me? When was happiness a bad thing? "And this was detrimental?"

"It was terrible," she said seriously. "Horrible. The worst thing that could possibly have occurred."

"How's that again?"

"This may be difficult to believe—"

"Oh, it is," I replied, still trying to wrap my head around the concept. "But try me."

Betty pulled her corncob pipe from her pocket, lit it with a flame that burst from her finger, and started puffing away. "Happiness is a good thing, don't get me wrong. But there is such a thing as having too much of it."

Impossible, but I kept my thoughts to myself, letting her speak her truth.

"If one has too much of it, there's nothing else to do, nothing else to achieve. It's as if happiness is the pinnacle of human emotion. If that's all that fills a person, then they're doomed."

"I'm still not understanding."

I was also beginning to be worried, because we'd been absent from the group for a while. Surely Mullins Rob had noticed our vacancy by now. He'd be worried, wondering where we were. We needed to wrap this up and get back to them.

"Don't you see?" Betty said, exasperated. "If you have too much joy, then you won't strive or want anything else. You could be out of food, starving, but you'd be happy, so it wouldn't matter. Or even worse, your children could be starving but they wouldn't care, and neither would you. You wouldn't even be sad when they died."

The truth of it was shocking. Now I understood. This curse was worse than one that made a person miserable or cursed them with a deformity. It was a wolf-in-sheep's-clothing spell, the ultimate evil made to look sweet and harmless. This was true evil.

Who came up with this stuff, anyway? What sort of sick minds were in the world that someone thought to give others the curse of happiness? Did they do it just to watch others be so happy that they died miserable yet joyful deaths? I didn't know, but one thing was for sure. Evil knew no limits.

I asked the most obvious question. "How did you stop it?"

"I didn't," came the sharp reply. "The one person who wasn't affected by the curse was your mother."

Blood pooled at my feet. My mouth went drier than a desert. My mother had saved the town? She'd been the only person unaffected?

"How?" I asked.

"She'd snuck out to see a human boy the night the witch unleashed it on us."

"My father?"

"Your father." Betty nodded sharply. "When she returned, we were all under the spell. Your mother, smart one that she was, figured out what was going on and was able to contain the curse here, under this wall. It couldn't be destroyed. It couldn't be bottled or sent away. This was what she did, saving us all."

"Wow," was all I could think to say.

Betty laid a hand on the brick. "That's why it was so important for me to make sure that this was intact. If the magic behind these rocks was ever unleashed…well, I don't know who would be around to save us. We almost didn't survive the assault the first time. We probably wouldn't last the second."

I shivered at how close we stood to such powerful magic. Betty had been right to want to check on it. The idea that this wall could be destroyed by one swing of the alligator's tail, sending us all into a spiral of death, was more than unnerving. It was downright stomach twisting.

"Can we move the spell?" I asked. "Put it back in the Vault?"

Betty shook her head. "That, I don't know. We'd have to have the help of other wizards. Axel would be a good one to ask. We can do that."

Oh no. She couldn't ask him. It was time to tell her what was going on. "Betty, Axel isn't Axel."

She inhaled deeply from her pipe before releasing the smoke into the air, where it dissipated against the brick wall. "You think he's Adam."

"He was seen in two places at once." I found myself pleading with her, wanting her to so desperately believe what I did. "You and I both know what sort of magic that is."

"Cordelia told me all about it."

"She thinks I'm crazy."

"I don't. I've been watching him. He seems a little off."

A gush of air left my lungs in relief. "You believe me?"

"I do. Saw him scratching the back of his neck. Axel never scratches. He rubs. It's not one of his tics."

My husband had tics? Not like the insect kind, but the character kind? Since when was Betty such an astute student of people's movements? I didn't care because right now it was all working in my favor.

"So you believe that my husband is missing?"

Betty rubbed her chin. "Yep, and we've got to find him."

"That's why I was down here. I figured it was a good spot for Adam to hide him."

Betty was quiet for a long moment. I feared she was thinking the worst, that something terrible had happened to Axel. When she did speak, her words made me feel better.

"We've got to draw him out," she told me.

"How?"

"I'll ask Shoo. We'll need help for this. But don't worry, we'll get your husband back, 'cause I don't believe Adam's harmed him. He ain't that stupid. Adam needs Axel alive to make sure that he's saying the right things, doing the right things, acting the correct way in order to assimilate into his brother's life."

I'd wanted to keep this on the down low, but if only a few more people knew, maybe that would be okay. I couldn't do this all by myself, not while being a mom. Plus, I couldn't even allow myself to grieve or be angry. The weight of thinking that something bad had happened to Axel was too much; it was more than I could take.

"What's your plan?" I asked.

Just then, sounds of men shouting caught our attention. Betty and I rushed toward the voices, momentarily putting our conversation aside.

I heard Mullins Rob's voice break over the others. "It's here," he yelled. "The alligator! Get him, fellas!"

CHAPTER 12

I started to take off down the tunnel but stopped. Betty couldn't run as fast as me.

She smirked. "You waiting for an old lady?"

"Um, well, yeah," I told her with tons of shame in my words. There was no hiding it. It was embarrassing to even say it, though it was true. "I don't want to leave you behind."

She cackled. "You should know by now that you don't have to worry about me, kid."

With that, Betty held a finger over one nostril. Magic uncoiled from her open nasal passage and snapped at her feet like a whip.

"Giddy up," Betty called. "I'm right behind you."

Without waiting another moment, I took off, racing down the corridor. Within seconds, Betty was charging past me, her feet a blur as she raced down the tunnel. Would it have been too much to ask for her to help me out a little bit?

There she was, shooting through the sewers at a good fifty miles per hour while I was stuck pedaling at regular human speed, whatever that was.

But my grandmother didn't seem to think I needed any extra help. Either that or she wanted all the glory, and to reach Mullins Rob first, because the next thing I knew, she'd disappeared from view. She was gone, out of sight, and I was stuck trying to follow the sounds of the men yelling as I made my way toward them.

Finally, after what felt like forever, I reached the clot of police officers, Adam and Betty, who I swore gave me a triumphant look.

Why was she proud for beating me? When you became old and crotchety, was there very little left in life that made you happy, so that when you bested your granddaughter at running, it became a clear victory for you?

Perhaps.

It would be a few decades before I found that out.

"Where's the alligator?" I asked.

Mullins Rob shot me a look so scathing I was surprised that I had any skin left on my bones. What had *I* done?

"Yeah, we found the gator," he snarled.

Again, I couldn't help but feel that his ire was pinned on me. And once again, as far as I knew, my only sin was in telling the sheriff that there was a gator in these here parts.

But then Mullins moved aside and there, attached to the wall, looked like an alligator skin. I squinted, unsure if I was seeing the thing right. There was light in the sewer, thanks to magic, but the tunnels were still rather dim. It wasn't like Adam had brought the sun down with him when he came, though I have to admit, when Mullins asked him to light our path, the imposter had done a very good job at it.

Almost too good.

Anyhow, back to the beast. Slowly, and full of hesitation, I made my way to the wall, where the thing hung. The closer I got, the stranger it looked. The gator's scales looked to be painted on.

I gasped. "It's a costume."

"A costume," Mullins croaked, "hanging on a wall. That was the gator you saw."

The men and even Betty glared at me something fierce, as if I were an evil supervillain who'd just tricked all of them and had stolen their powers.

But I *had* seen an alligator. It had charged after me. "No," I argued. "That's not what was here last night. I swear it. There was a gator. It raced after me. I had to escape it. I promise you."

Mullins placed his hands on his hips and spoke to Adam. "I don't want to say that I know what's going on with your wife, but it seems to me that maybe she should get some rest."

"No," I screeched. Why was everyone telling me that I was cracking up? I wasn't cracking up. I shot a pleading look to Betty, who took my hand.

"There, there," my grandmother cooed. "Why don't we get out of here? Let you get some sleep."

"But I don't need to."

"Now, now." Betty pulled me away from the huddled group of men and whispered, "Just do as I say. We'll work this out."

"Okay," I said quietly.

I turned back, I don't know why, I think out of instinct. Adam looked so much like Axel it was hard to believe that the man standing with Mullins Rob wasn't my husband. But if I'd had any doubt as to his real identity, it was laid to rest in that moment. For the man acting like my husband didn't look to be concerned for me at all. His entire focus was on the men and the alligator suit that they had found.

~

BETTY GOT me back to her house, where Amelia was watching Gizzy. *Gizzy.* With everything that had happened, I'd nearly forgotten about my daughter.

She was playing on the floor with Amelia, sitting upright and building those core muscles. My cousin was putting toys just out of her reach so that the baby had to work to grab them.

Amelia's eyes flashed with worry when she spotted Betty leading me in. "What's wrong? Pepper, you look terrible."

"That's not what your cousin needs to hear right now," Betty snapped. "She needs your support."

"Oh, okay." Amelia rose and helped me to the couch, where I slumped on top of it.

"I'll make you some tea," Betty announced.

She headed over to the everlasting fire crackling in the hearth. There, she pinched bits of dried lavender and chamomile from where it hung on the mantel and ground them between her hands before dropping them into a kettle. She set the kettle on an iron arm above the fire and sat in her rocker, eyeing me.

"You sure what you saw was an alligator?"

I swallowed a knot in my throat. It *had* been an alligator, hadn't it? Now I was beginning to doubt myself. No. I couldn't do that. It was what Adam wanted, because he was the person behind all of this, wasn't he?

"Pepper?" Betty prodded when I didn't answer.

"Yes," I said, lifting my gaze to meet hers. "It was an alligator. It charged at me through the sewer and would have eaten me if I hadn't, at the last minute, magicked myself out of there. I know it sounds crazy. I know that everything I've said sounds insane, but I'm not hallucinating. *Please.* You've got to believe me."

The kettle screeched as steam poured from the spout. Betty wiggled from the chair, grabbed a mitt and pulled the kettle from the flames. With the snap of her fingers, three teacups appeared and she filled each of them to the brim with the liquid.

Two cups glided over to me and Amelia. It was too hot to drink, so I motioned for it to settle on an end table beside me.

Amelia spoke. "You know, there's a lot of pressure on me, too. This whole wedding deal is beginning to give me a huge headache. From finding a venue to picking out the cake, it's madness. I've almost felt myself about to crack up several times, and I even have the book to guide me."

"I'm not cracking up," I insisted. "Look, I know that I lost nearly all my animals and managed to find that one kitten." I bolted up. "The kitten! She knows about the alligator. She can confirm it. She was there. Although maybe she slept through the entire attack."

Betty sipped her steaming tea. I have no idea how because it was still too hot to drink. I'm sure it must've burnt off a few of her taste buds in the process.

"I believe you," she told me, "about the alligator."

I nearly jumped from my seat. "You do?"

"Yes, same as I believe you about Adam taking Axel's place."

"What?" Amelia said. "What's this?"

I sighed. Couldn't someone have filled my cousin in on everything that was going on? Then again, Cordelia might've told her, but Amelia was probably too busy deciding what colored napkins to have at the reception to remember.

So I took a brief two minutes and explained everything. She listened quietly, her eyes widening to plates as I went on.

"So what about the creature?" she asked when I had finished.

It sounded so insane, but I had to say it. "I think that Adam placed it there to cover up his tracks."

"And what about Axel?" she asked.

"He moved him," Betty said flatly.

Hope rose in my chest. "You think so."

"Must have. Otherwise it doesn't make sense. An alligator costume didn't attack you last night. It was an alligator, pure and simple. But that gator is gone. Mullins checked all over those sewers when we slipped away."

Amelia's eyes narrowed. "Why'd y'all slip away?"

"No reason," Betty mumbled. "But they didn't see the beast. Why?"

"Because it wasn't there," I said. "Because someone had moved it."

"Precisely," Betty said with the jab of her finger. "Someone, namely that man who's pretending to be your husband, vanished it. Why?"

I sipped my tea, which had cooled to just below scalding, and considered her question. Why would Adam have moved the alligator? I'd thought that perhaps the creature and Adam weren't related at first, but now that seemed unlikely. That there was a connection between the two seemed the most obvious explanation as to what was going on. Why else would the beast have been absent from the sewers?

It was Amelia who spoke first. "You went to the sewers in the first place to find Axel, right?"

"Right," I said, still sipping the tea, which was relaxing me more and more as I drank it. "That's what happened."

"Well," she replied slowly as if still chewing on the idea, "what if the alligator was put in place to guard Axel, to make sure that no one found him?"

"Betty?" I asked. "What do you think? Could that have been it?"

"Amelia." She said my cousin's name darkly, as if she was about to scold her for even entertaining the notion that Adam could have been using the creature as a soldier in his diabolical plan. That was where I thought she was going, but then Betty smiled widely. "You're a genius."

Amelia beamed. It wasn't often that anyone called her a genius. "You think it's possible?"

"I know it is," Betty said, energy bubbling from her. My grandmother rose and paced in front of the fire. "It makes the most sense. How else did an alligator get down into the sewers? It couldn't have done so by itself unless it escaped a pet store. Pepper, you've never had baby alligators for sale as familiars, have you?"

"No," I told them. "But I have to say, the kitten told me that other animals were in the sewers." Tears pricked my eyes. "You don't think the gator ate them, do you?"

Oh no, it had! That beast had eaten all my animals. My heart sank at the very thought that my puppies and kittens had come to such a horrible end.

Amelia patted my shoulder. "Those animals are small and wily. They wouldn't have simply walked into that alligator's jaws. They're probably still there, hiding. I know it."

I knuckled away tears that had dripped onto my cheeks. "You think so?"

She smiled tenderly. "I know so. But. What are we going to do about finding the alligator and Axel now? We can't let Adam know that we're on to him. We have to keep everything on the down low."

Betty stroked her chin. "Ladies, I've got just the plan."

I couldn't wait to hear this.

CHAPTER 13

Betty's plan turned out to be fairly simple—keep Gizzy at her house in order to ensure her safety by telling Adam that I was too busy trying to put my shop back together to watch her and that Betty had asked if her great-granddaughter could sleep over a few nights.

That was the first and easiest part of the plan. However, we couldn't let Adam think that anything was up, which meant that I had to act normally. So I had to be his wife, for all intents and purposes.

But in the meantime we also needed to find Axel, the *real* Axel. So when I wasn't at my home or at Familiar Place, I needed to be figuring out exactly where Adam had stowed my husband. Or, as Betty also informed me, I could attempt to seduce the information out of Adam. Like I was a KGB spy or something. Who did Betty think I was?

When I asked her that, she told me I was a desperate woman. I'd lost my creatures to Adam. I wouldn't lose my husband to him as well.

So we came up with this plan, and I was about to head home when an idea struck me. "Amelia, can I borrow your cast-iron skillet?"

"Sure. It's by the door."

I took it from its place and hoisted it up. "I'll bring it back tomorrow."

She waved me away. "No rush. It's not as if I'll be riding it down the aisle or anything."

Huh. That would be interesting, but I didn't need to give her any other ideas to ponder over when it came to her nuptials. So I took the skillet and left, heading for the Cobweb Forest.

I found Ross and Ellen's house easily enough, even though I was convinced that the trees were purposely attempting to hide it from me. I swore, those oaks and pines in the forest could be so wily it was annoying.

But anyhow, I landed in their front yard and knocked on the door. Ross answered. His shirt wasn't opened this time, I noted.

"Hi, Pepper. Come on in." He was all smiles as I entered. "Can I get you something to drink? I've got coffee."

"Um, no thanks. I was actually wondering if Ellen was around?"

He shook his head. "I'm sorry to say that she's not. Went off to see her aunt again. She'll be back tonight, though." He went to the fridge and pulled out a water bottle, handing it to me even though I'd told him that I didn't need anything. Such a conscientious person. "Do you want me to give her a message?"

"Well, um, I was wondering if she told you that I saw her last night?"

His brows peaked and he quickly said, "Yes, she did."

"I saw her right after leaving the sewer. I'd told her about the alligator, and to be honest, she didn't seem all that rattled by it. Not like I had been."

"Oh, right. Well"—he chuckled—"alligators don't disturb my wife. She's used to seeing all sorts of magical beasts."

I couldn't help but to lift my own brows. "Is that so?"

"Yeah, she used to track them down but retired from it."

"Is that why she was out in town last night?"

"Er, um." He grabbed a water, unscrewed it and took a long drink, obviously looking for time. "That's the way she comes home from her aunt's. She goes through town and then makes her way here."

"The reason why I'm asking is because I'm wondering if she saw something else."

"What sort of something else?" His words were casual, but his tone wasn't. "What do you mean?"

"I was wondering if, perhaps, she saw the alligator leave, or someone else wandering around outside?"

"How could an alligator have left?" he asked sharply.

"Oh, it wouldn't have. I mean, they can't climb," I replied, laughing nervously. "But anyway, I thought to ask."

He shrugged. "Are you sure what you saw was an alligator?"

Why was he questioning what it was that I had seen? Why would it matter to Ross?

I smiled tightly. "I'm sure. But anyway, do you have her number so that I can call her?"

"I gave it to your husband last time," he said, annoyed.

Well since then, my husband's disappeared, did not seem like the right way to respond. "We lost it. Sorry."

"No problem," he told me. Ross was smiling again as he gave me her digits. "Thanks."

I left the house, tucking the water bottle into my back pocket. As soon as Ross shut the door behind me, I dialed Ellen's number.

She never answered, and I left a message. But strangely enough, I swore that from inside the house, I heard her phone ringing.

Now why would Ellen's phone be inside the house if she was at her aunt's? And if that was the case, why hadn't Ross just told me that?

This mystery just kept getting deeper and deeper. I prayed that before I solved it, that it didn't drown the life from me.

CHAPTER 14

I got home and started making supper. I wasn't a great cook, but there were about three things that I could make well. One of them was a spaghetti bake. I hardly ever put it together because it was a lot of carbs and Axel complained that it would make him fat. Personally I didn't believe that anything could make my husband fat. He was perfect.

But I wasn't dealing with my husband, now was I? I was dealing with Adam, and he could wind up weighing as much as a two-story building for all I cared.

With Betty watching Gizzy, the house was eerily quiet, so quiet that I put on some music while I gathered the ingredients.

"What are you doing?" Mattie asked from her sun-drenched spot on the floor.

"Oh!" I tossed a pot into the air in fright, barely having time to zap it back into my hands before it clattered to the floor. "I didn't see you there. You nearly scared me half to death."

She yawned. "You were too busy humming to yourself to see me." Mattie's ears swiveled like satellites atop her head. "I don't hear the baby. What you got going on?"

"Oh, I'm having a special dinner with Axel."

"I see. What're you making?"

"Spaghetti bake."

"It'll make him fat," she argued.

"Let's just say, I'm not worried about that."

She sat up and eyed me suspiciously. "Why not? He's complained about it before."

I shrugged as I waved my hand and the pot moved to the sink. The faucet turned on, and water filled the container. "Axel's not going to gain any weight. You know how much he works out, and he eats really well most of the time."

"Something's going on. Pepper, what is it?"

"Nothing."

"You're lying."

My grandmother and cousins already knew my suspicions. It wouldn't be right if everyone on God's green earth knew what I suspected. The information would get back to Adam and then goodness knew what would happen to Axel.

No. It was best if I kept some information to myself. So in answer to Mattie's question, I scoffed. "You're putting words in my mouth. I just think Axel's been acting a little funny lately, so I thought that I'd cheer him up with this dish."

"He keeping something from you, sugar?"

"I'm sorry?" How could the cat hit the nail on the head so quickly? "Hiding something? No, not at all."

She sat up and stretched her legs in front of her. "In that case, you need to work a truth potion on him."

Now she had my attention. "Truth potion? What are you talking about?"

"I'm talking about the fact that you could work one on him to find out what it is that you want to know. It might be better than baking him a spaghetti that'll just make him fat."

"It won't make him fat." She gave me a stern look. "Okay, it *won't* make him fat unless he eats too much of it."

"That's better."

"But what about this truth serum are you talking about?"

"Oh, so you're interested?"

"I wouldn't say that."

She lifted her nose. "Then I won't tell you about it."

"Mattie, please." Gosh, why did I sound so desperate? "I'd like to know. The truth is...I do think that Axel's keeping something from me. There's some information I need. Just a few answers, that's all. Nothing big. It's something tiny."

It felt horrible to lie to my cat. I mean, really horrible. Who was I to lie to Mattie, someone who was kind and wonderful to me?

But like I'd already said, it was best if more folks or even animals didn't know. I was only protecting her, in a way. The less she knew, the better.

She jumped up onto the kitchen counter. "You want me to teach you a truth potion?"

"Yes, but I'm almost afraid to ask how you know the recipe."

"Oh, that's no big deal. Your mama used to dose Betty every once in a while to find out the truth on what she really thought of her boyfriends."

"What?" I shrieked. "Mama used to give Betty truth serum?"

Mattie laughed. "That surprise you?"

"Well, yes. It does. A lot. I can't imagine putting a spell on Betty. I'm pretty sure she'd sniff it out in a second and then would spank my butt for it."

Mattie chuckled hard. "Yeah, that happened a few times, too. Your mama was nearly grown and she'd have to find the switch that Betty was going to use to spank her with."

"Oh my goodness. Well, maybe I shouldn't do the truth serum."

"No, it works. Works as good as they come, and totally tasteless." She made a hook with the end of her tail. "Unless, of course, you don't want to."

No, I wanted to. This would be the fastest, easiest way to discover that Adam was Axel. Once I had proof, I could go to Sheriff Rob and explain what happened. Then the sheriff would take him prisoner and torture him until Adam revealed where he was hiding Axel.

Hmm. I liked this plan. I liked it a lot.

"All right, tell me the ingredients."

Mattie grinned, revealing small, pointy canines. "We can do it while your spaghetti bakes. Now let's get started."

After I'd made the spaghetti, mixed in all the ingredients and got it baking, Mattie instructed me on the serum. There were eggshells to throw in and a frog's eye, a crow's feather and snakeskin. All of those I found in Axel's magic room. Then I had to distill peacock feathers down to get the dye. That took the longest. Getting the color from the fibers was tedious, hard work. If the feather soaked too long in alcohol, then the dye would be ruined, and if it didn't soak long enough, then the color wouldn't have the full saturation that it needed.

But Mattie instructed me perfectly, and I was able to extract the exact hue. From there, I put all the ingredients together, mixing them with the mortar and pestle until they were dust.

"And the last thing you need is blood."

I groaned. "Why does this spell require blood? But of course it does because there always has to be a little pain in when you actually need some information. Magic is so annoying."

Mattie rolled her eyes. "Quit your yammering. It's not like you're using it to summon a demon or anything. This ain't that big a deal. Just a little cut. You gave birth, didn't you? You can give up some of your plasma."

When she put it that way, my cat made me sound like a big old wuss. So I took a knife and made a small cut in the hill of my hand, watching as the blood dripped into the cup of the mortar.

As soon as the liquid came into contact with the ingredients, it hissed and gray smoke curled from the bowl.

"Now to bind the spell, you need to say these words," my cat told me.

I repeated the chant, and the ingredients hissed louder and bubbled. Were we making a truth serum or poison? But I trusted Mattie, so I remained on course, repeating the words that I was supposed to. When it all was said and done, the egg shell, feather, skin and everything else congealed, forming into a clear liquid. You couldn't even tell that I'd steeped part of a peacock feather in alcohol. Why had I even done that if the serum wasn't going to be blue? But I supposed that didn't matter.

"Now pour it into a vial, something to hold it," she instructed.

I had expected this and had retrieved a small vial from Axel's workroom. I didn't breathe as I transferred the liquid into the clear container, holding my lungs to make sure that I didn't move and spill the potion.

When it was done, I exhaled. "There."

"You'll need to use the whole vial, every drop," Mattie told me.

"Got it." My gaze wandered to the clock. It was getting late. Adam would be home any minute. "Now time to clean up the mess."

I quickly washed and put everything away, back where I had found the ingredients. Even if Adam had inspected Axel's workroom carefully, he wouldn't notice that some things were missing. I'd been sure to only take the smallest of ingredients and after that, to move the egg shells and snake skins around to make it look like the jars were full, untouched, as it were.

Just as I finished up, the timer on the oven went off (yes, I still cooked the old-fashioned way) and the front door opened. Mattie quickly raced to the living room in order to look innocent, and I pointed my finger at the fireplace and *vroom!* a fire lit in the hearth.

"Hey," Adam called. "I'm home."

"I'm just in here finishing up dinner."

He walked in looking all buff and very Axel-like. It was super annoying. He gave me a wicked grin. "Something smells delicious."

"It's spaghetti bake," I said, raising my brow, waiting for him to fail his first test. That was one of his favorites, as I'd mentioned. Okay, so he complained that it would make him fat, but deep down, Axel loved it. Fussing about it was just his way of telling me that he didn't want to eat too much because he would pack on the pounds.

He rubbed his hands. "Wow, you cooked that for me? Looks like you went to a lot of trouble." Before I could answer, he kissed my forehead and brushed past me, heading for the living room, where he fell into a chair. Then he stopped and glanced around. "Where's Gizzy?"

"At Betty's. I thought we could use an evening alone."

He rubbed the back of his neck. "Is something wrong?"

"No, no," I replied quickly. "Nothing's wrong. It's just with the store and the sewer and everything, I'm really tired."

"Yeah."

Wasn't he going to comment on the sewer? Or the alligator skin? Axel would have. He would have said something, anything about it. Adam was doing a horrible job at imitating my husband.

I waited for him to say something, but when he flipped on the television and started to zone out, I chirped, "Ready to eat? I'll bring a plate for you in here."

"That would be great."

I heaped two big spoonfuls of the bake onto two plates. Very carefully and quietly, I opened the vial holding the potion and soaked the plate on my right. I picked it up and said, "What would you like to drink?"

"What's that?"

He wasn't that far away, but Adam also didn't turn around to hear me. He was so lazy. I couldn't wait to get my husband back. Axel wouldn't just sit in front of the television talking to me over his shoulder; he would tell me that he loved my fattening spaghetti bake and couldn't wait to sink his werewolf teeth into it.

Annoyed, I lowered the plate and marched over to him. "I said, what would you like to drink?"

He dragged his gaze from the television and glanced up at me. "Um, water's fine. Thanks."

Fuming, I stalked back into the kitchen and poured him a glass of water. Then I moved to grab his plate and stopped.

Crap.

Which one had I dosed?

I'd been so annoyed with how inconsiderate he was being that I'd forgotten to pay attention to where I'd placed the platter of food. The two still sat beside one another, but which was which? Was it the one on the right or the one on the left?

The left. Definitely the left. I picked it up along with the glass of water, steeled myself and headed to the living room.

There was no turning back now.

CHAPTER 15

"How's your supper?" I asked after Adam had taken a few bites.

"Good," he murmured, gaze glued to the television.

If there had ever been any doubt that this wasn't my husband, it was gone now. Axel would've been praising the heck out of my cooking.

How long did it take for the truth serum to kick in? Silly me, I'd forgotten to ask, so I shot Mattie a look.

She lay on the floor, curled up by the fire. What the heck? Couldn't she lift her head or something? But she was clearly down for the count, seduced by the warmth of the blaze.

Okay, I needed to know if the potion had kicked in, so I would start out easy, by asking small questions.

"So what did you do today?" I asked, fully expecting Adam to reply something about wanting to take over the world.

Boy, if he did that, then my job would be done.

But that wasn't what he said. Instead he replied, "Worked on that monster hunting research."

Huh. So apparently Adam was taking his role as Axel seriously. Okay. Two could play at this game. "Why do you think someone assaulted my store?"

His gaze darted to me in question before quickly focusing back on the television. "To get back at you for something. You've put lots of people in prison."

"Including your brother."

"Yep."

"What if your brother wasn't in prison anymore?" This was it. What I'd said was open-ended enough that Adam could wind his way into telling me the truth. All he had to do was really listen and he'd end up revealing that he was, in fact, Adam. All he had to do was say it.

Come on.

"Huh?" he asked.

I nearly smacked myself in the forehead. He hadn't even been listening? "Let's play a game. I ask you a question, and then you ask me a question."

"Do we have to? I'm tired tonight. I just want to eat and relax. It's not you. There's a lot going on with work."

"Since when is there a lot going on there? Usually whatever you've got going on, you keep there."

He laid his fork on the plate. "Do you want the truth?"

Mattie sat up. Now she decided to pay attention. Where had she been two minutes earlier?

"Yes, I want the truth." I could hardly contain my excitement. "That would be great."

"The truth is...I'm worried about you."

Oh, no. Not this again.

"I've been doing some work trying to figure out if something's going on, some spell that could've affected you, made you see that alligator costume as a real creature."

"It was a real alligator! It wasn't a prop or a figment of my imagination. It was real. I swear it. The creature was running, chasing me." Steam was about to pour from my ears I was so angry. "Tell me the truth—what were you doing today?"

He sighed, rubbed his eyes. "I've told you. Researching monsters to see if any have hallucinogenic affects."

Who was he? Was Adam immune to the effects of the potion? Or perhaps this was true. He was researching monsters for his own purposes, his own evil machinations. That would make sense. If he was the one who put the alligator into the sewers, then he'd need to make sure that he could use its power to the fullest extent.

It made perfect sense, and it also meant that Adam was still being honest. The truth serum was working! Great. That was what I needed. I had to get him to tell me more, to really give me the dirty details. I could simply just come out and ask him if he was Adam. It was the only way. I could contain him, I knew that. The power simmered within me. He was strong and had magic, but I could best him if I had to. After all, they didn't let you practice magic in prison, so he was probably rusty.

But the fact that he'd captured my husband and then managed to create an alligator also told me he must've had a lot of reserve power at his fingertips. This wouldn't be an easy victory, but it could be dòne.

First, I needed a quick plan. Once I asked him the question and Adam revealed his true identity, I would need to hold him. The best way to do that was to contain him with a force field. If he broke free of it, then he was a greater challenge than I anticipated, which meant I'd need to flee.

My cast-iron skillet was propped by the back door. If I was quick, there'd be time to magic Mattie away, grab the broom and race out the door and into the sky for safety.

I could be at Betty's within a matter of minutes to warn everyone.

Or if he broke free, I could grab Mattie and just make a portal and go through it.

Perhaps that was the easiest and best plan.

All right. This was it. As the question formed on my lips, Adam asked over his shoulder, "This is good. What's in it, again?"

"Oh," I felt myself answering, "it's just noodles, meat, sauce, spices, and truth serum."

My hand flew to my mouth. Oops. I hadn't dosed Adam at all. I'd taken the truth serum myself!

CHAPTER 16

Well, that had not gone the way that I'd anticipated. Of course, who anticipates dosing themselves with truth serum when your entire intention is to dose the other person? The one who actually must tell the truth?

I didn't need to be spilling any beans, because I didn't have any to spill. But Adam, he had a ton of beans to reveal.

But anyway, when I told him what was actually in the spaghetti bake, he wasn't listening, so he didn't even hear me say the words *truth serum*. See? Just another reason to know that he wasn't my husband, that he was an imposter. Right then and there I got up and cleaned the kitchen. I didn't want to give him another excuse to ask me what was in the bake and me end up telling him again. What if he heard the next time? Then I would have been in deep trouble.

Adam went to bed early, complaining that researching monsters made him tired. *Right.* How was reading a book all day tiring? It wasn't. He was such a bad liar.

Whereas books didn't make one fatigued, truth serum did, because it wasn't but a few minutes later that I was overcome with sleep. Exhausted, I magicked up a pair of pajamas and fell atop the couch, instantly dissolving into a deep slumber.

When I awoke, sunlight was brightening the windows and birds were chirping outside. Adam came downstairs carrying the scent of a magical spring with him (that was his washing soap).

"You slept down here?"

I yawned. "Yeah. Fell asleep watching TV." I was a good liar under duress. "But I'm up now."

"Want some breakfast?"

He opened the refrigerator door and started pulling out vegetables to make a disgusting green shake. Adam must have had the same obsession with gross breakfast shakes that Axel did.

"No thanks. I'm good. I'm going to shower and get going."

"Oh? What are you up to today?" he asked.

Why was it that normally I never would've thought the question to mean anything deep? But when Adam asked it, I wasn't sure how to answer because it felt like my response was being measured, weighed.

Well, the truth was always the best, as my dad would have said. So that was what I gave him. "I'm going to see if I can find any more of my animals. If not, I guess I'll just order some. After all, I can't have an empty familiar store, now can I?"

"No, I suppose you can't."

I went upstairs and got ready. By the time I came back down, Adam had gone and Mattie was licking up a bit of breakfast shake that had spilled onto the floor.

"Ugh. You like that stuff?"

"It tastes better than truth serum," she said with a snort.

"Very funny. I'll have you know that it was an accident that I dosed myself."

She ran her tongue along the edges of her mouth. "I didn't think you'd done it on purpose."

"Well, now you know."

"And knowing is half the battle."

"Okay, G.I. Joe," I said, referring to an old 1980's cartoon. "I need to get going. See you tonight."

"See you then."

I headed to Betty's to pick up the kitten that I'd left there and to check on Gizzy. She was doing great. Amelia was watching her as Betty had some things that she needed to take care of. Amelia wouldn't tell me what, which made me wonder if my grandmother was up to illegal activities. If she was, there was good reason for it.

I deposited the kitten at Familiar Place and spent fifteen minutes grilling her on the whereabouts of the other animals, but all I could get out of her was that they'd been in the sewer with her and that she'd lost track of them.

But here was the thing—they couldn't have been in the tunnels anymore. No, I didn't think so, because when I'd gone down with Mullins Rob, no one had seen hide nor hair of them. That could only mean that the creatures had gotten out of the tunnels and this one kitten had been left behind. Or they'd been eaten, but I didn't want to even consider that possibility.

But if they were still in the sewers, maybe they were at the very edges of the tunnels, where we hadn't checked. What I needed was a map of the tunnels, a way to know where I'd been and what I'd seen.

The only way to get that would be to get it from the city, and the place who would have access to that was the mayor's office.

All right, mayor of Magnolia Cove, here I came.

~

GILDA GOLDENHEART WAS a woman I was very familiar with, though I rarely encountered. She wasn't someone who I spoke to on a weekly, nor even a monthly basis, but that didn't mean that the mayor wasn't nice when she saw me standing outside her office.

"Well, Pepper Dunn, I mean, Reign. Honey, how're you doing?"

Gilda, who had a breathy quality to her voice, looked like what you'd think an older lady would—her hair was curly, she wore big glasses with plastic frames, a shirt with a cardigan over it and lots of jewelry that clinked together when she walked.

Her ankles were puffy over her pumps, and I wondered if she tossed her shoes off when her office door was closed. I knew that I would, but I said nothing, just accepted the embrace that she offered.

"Come in," she said, pointing to a chair on the other side of her desk. "Now, what can I do for you?"

"I need a favor."

Her brows lifted. "Well, I don't know about favors, but honey, I'll do whatever for you that I can."

I wasn't sure what that meant, but I forged ahead anyway. "Great. You know that my store was broken into."

"Honey, I heard about that and it's terrible. I just can't believe that someone in Magnolia Cove would do such a terrible thing."

"Me neither. It is awful. I agree. But I found one of my kittens."

"Well, that's wonderful." Gilda sat up and rested her elbows on the desk. "And is she okay?"

"Yes, she's fine. Just fine. But here's the thing—I found her in the sewers."

"Oh, goodness." She clutched the gold necklace at her throat. Her name wasn't Gilda for nothing. "Honey, that's just about the worst thing I've ever heard."

Which part? The part about me being in the sewers or the cat in there? Though I was tempted to ask, I bit my tongue. "She said there were others there, and I need to find them. Which means that I need a favor."

"Yes, yes. Tell me. I'll help you with anything."

Here went nothing. "I need a map of the sewers so that I can go down there and locate the rest."

"Oh." She slumped back onto her seat. "Honey, I'll be honest with you."

"Yes?" Excitement sparked in my chest. Maybe her being honest would be in my favor. "I'd love that."

"Good, because I considered having you arrested after it was discovered that you went into the sewers alone a few days ago."

Oh. This was not the kind of honest that I'd been expecting. "I'm sorry?"

"I already knew about your little jaunt. Mullins Rob told me. Don't you just love our new sheriff?"

"Sometimes," I mumbled. Not when he was tattletaling on me, though.

"Honey, I had to sign an official order so that he could search those sewers. No one's supposed to be in them except for official Magnolia Cove people."

"And I suppose that I'm not one of those?" I squeaked out.

"I hate to say it, but no, you're not. Now, I know that you've done a lot for this community. You continue to do so much for it, and I would love to help you if I could. But if folks discovered that I gave you special privileges, then they would expect that I'd give everyone those same privileges, and that's not how you run a town."

How did she run this town to begin with? Because I literally never saw her out and about. Was Gilda even sure that she was running the town at all? Was there another person, a man behind the proverbial curtain, so to speak, that was actually moving the levers of Magnolia Cove?

Okay, I was being ridiculous. There wasn't anyone else sitting in her chair.

"So you're not going to give me the map?" I asked.

She pressed a hand to her chest. "As much as I would love to, I can't. It's against the office's policy. If you need someone to search for you, ask the sheriff and then he'll come to me. Otherwise there's nothing I can do, honey. My hands are tied."

I rose and thanked her. "Well, I appreciate you taking the time to see me."

"Anytime, honey, anytime. You're always welcome here."

I left the mayor's office feeling discouraged. There were so many questions going on in my mind. How was I going to prove that Adam had done something to Axel? Where were my animals? I knew that I'd seen an alligator in the tunnels. Why was someone (Adam) trying to make me look like a liar?

Okay, that one had an easy explanation—to cover his tracks, of course. That was the most likely reason.

I needed help. I needed Betty. I pulled my phone from my purse and called her cell but didn't receive an answer. Great. She was incommunicado.

As I walked down Bubbling Cauldron Road, completely unsure what my next steps would be, I noticed a bird chirping nearby. It was a little wren, and every time I took a step, the bird jumped onto a nearby tree branch, singing the whole time.

"If only you had answers for me, little bird," I murmured, not too loudly so that people walking by wouldn't think I was crazy. Or at least they wouldn't think I was any crazier than I already was.

I sat on a bench, and the bird kept chittering. It flew down from its branch and jumped around on the sidewalk near me, talking away.

It was really unfortunate that the bird had so much to communicate, as I couldn't talk to it.

Or could I? Birds were hit-or-miss. Sometimes I could speak to them; sometimes I couldn't.

Hello, little bird, I told it telepathically.

Hello, it replied.

Oh, it could speak. Wonderful.

How're you? I mean, I had to be nice. I couldn't simply skip formalities. Also, I had no idea what to speak with the bird about.

Good. I know where your animals are.

Wait. What? *You do?*

How could this tiny wren know that? How could it be privy to that sort of information. And how did it know me?

The alligator isn't bad. Don't harm him.

Now the bird was talking about the alligator? How had we jumped from my animals to it? I didn't understand the connection. But I wasn't going to let that stop me from becoming the bird's new best friend.

Okay, I won't harm the alligator. Just as long as it doesn't try to eat me again. Ha ha.

He can't help himself.

He? It was a he? *Do you know him?*

Yes. You know him, too.

Wow. I knew him, too? But I didn't know anyone who was an alligator. She must've been talking about a shape-shifter. But I didn't know anyone who was one. Well, apart from Axel and the members of his clan. But Axel was a werewolf.

Who is he? I asked.

It's—

Just then my cell phone, which was still in my hand, blared to life, startling me. It fell, and I scrambled to pick it up before it smashed onto the ground.

Betty was calling me back. I swiped to answer. "Hold on a minute."

I looked back for the wren, to find out about the alligator, but the bird was gone.

It had vanished without a trace.

CHAPTER 17

I spoke to Betty. "Hey, what's going on?"

I was still distracted by the bird's leaving, so I barely heard my grandmother when she said, "I know where the alligator is."

"What?"

"The gator, kid. The one we're hunting. I know where the darned thing is hiding."

My heart jumped into my throat. "Where?"

"I'm up at the old settlement, near the mountains."

"Where the giants live?"

"Yep. Shoo's with me. Said he'd protect me."

Betty's boyfriend was all spindly legs and arms. I doubted very much that Shoo was capable of protecting anything bigger than a fly. "I'll be right there."

To make the trek to the mountains, I borrowed a cast-iron skillet from Harry and Theodora. Normally they cringed at such a thing because skillets were only paired with a particular person. But Harry had an all-purpose skillet that he was happy to loan me, though Theodora did a lot of grumbling about it.

But anyway, I arrived at the old settlement—and it was old, one of the original places that folks had made houses at when they first arrived in Magnolia Cove, but had deserted after a time.

There wasn't much left of the old settlement except for the original well. It looked just like you would have imagined—crumbling rocks and a circle of gray stone that was their old well. It still had the turning wheel and an old bucket dangling from a rope, so it wasn't completely unrecognizable.

"Howdie, Pepper," Shoo said in greeting.

I leaned the skillet against a tree trunk and crossed to him and Betty. "So you think the gator's up here?"

"Yep," Betty said. "Sure of it."

I glanced around the heavily wooded area. The ground was dry, the trees thick. This was not the ideal habitat for an alligator.

"Okay, where would it be? In the trees?"

Betty shook her head. "Nope. In there."

She pointed to the well. I laughed. "In the well?"

"Yep. That's it." My grandmother crossed to it. "My own grandmother told me that the well came from an underground river."

"And you think the alligator went in there? When there's the Potion Ponds it could've gone to."

"Nope, too many underwater creatures in those. The gator would've been kicked out sure as a wink. There's no telling where the underwater river leads to and what prey the gator could find there. But sure as shooting, I bet your Axel is down here, in a place where no one would ever think to look."

"Betty, it's too random. Adam wouldn't have dropped Axel all the way out here. How would he even know about it?"

She wiggled her brows. "Because he would've forced your husband to tell him about it."

She had a point, and what did we actually have to lose by diving in and searching? Not one darn thing, as far as I was concerned.

"Okay, let's do it." Betty magicked us to the bottom of the well, which was muddy as all get-out. "Ugh. This is worse than the sewers." I lifted one leg, which was nearly impossible as the mud was holding my foot like concrete. When I did manage to pull it out, a gross slurping sound ensued.

"I'll fix it," Betty announced. After a bit of magic flew from her nostrils, I found myself standing atop the mud, my shoes and jeans pristine. "There. Now we can search."

She conjured a floating flame and sent it on ahead to light our path. The underground river, I had to admit, was the perfect environment for an alligator. Well, if I was an alligator, I would have liked it.

It was dark with a good stream of water that was several feet deep, from what I could tell. Shoo had Betty make him a stick, and he pushed it down into the flowing liquid. When he pulled it back up, the stick was wet about two or three feet.

We followed the tunnel a good ways. It must've been close to half a mile before we reached a slope that we followed up and up until we were out in the sunlight. The river that had been so swift underground became a stream that became a trickle that turned into a spring that vanished into the dry ground.

I sighed. "Well, it was a good idea," I told Betty. "Thank you for trying. If Gilda had given me the blueprints to the sewers, I would've gone back there, but she told me that she wasn't going to do it. That she couldn't because it was illegal."

Betty's eyes narrowed. "Gilda said what?"

My grandmother's hostility took me by surprise. "Well, she said that I'd almost been arrested for going into the sewer in the first place. If I wound up back down there, then she'd have no choice but to throw me in jail."

Betty shot Shoo a look. "You thinking what I'm thinking?"

Shoo rubbed the scruffy hair on his chin. "That something stinks in Denmark?"

"I think the quote is that something's rotten in Denmark," I told them.

Betty ignored me. "It sounds to me like someone wants to keep you out of that sewer."

"Yeah, because it's illegal," I reminded her. "Gilda doesn't want me there because it's against the law."

"I don't believe that," she retorted. "Gilda doesn't care what folks do. Why should she give a beaver's butt whether or not you go into the sewers?"

I shrugged. "Well, maybe I could get hurt or fall and break my leg.

What if I couldn't get out? I mean, it could be a PR disaster for her if something like that happened."

"Nonsense. From the way you're talking, it sounds like they want to keep you out for a reason."

"They?" *Who was this they?* "Who are you talking about?"

With a sparkle in her eyes Betty replied, "I don't know, but we're about to find out."

∽

THAT NIGHT, we returned to the sewers. When I'd called Adam to let him know, he didn't seem all that concerned, which wasn't much of a surprise.

Of course, I didn't call and tell him that I was going to the sewers. No, that would've been stupid. The only thing he got out of me was that I was going to be late and if he wanted food, there was plenty of spaghetti bake left for him to eat.

I mean, he'd liked it so much he could eat on it for a few days as far as I was concerned.

But anyhow, Betty and I geared up for a night in the tunnels. Amelia was to watch the baby and Cordelia was nowhere to be seen—until the door flew open and there she was, coming in from work.

"Why're y'all dressed in black?" she asked.

We were, indeed, dressed in our commando best. The only thing we were missing were night-vision goggles. I was tempted to mention it to Betty (who'd been the one who created our outfits in the first place), but I decided to keep my mouth shut.

"For your information," Betty said, "we're going on a gator hunt."

Cordelia's eyes widened in surprise. I supposed that wasn't what she had expected to hear. But I was the one who became surprised when she said, "Can I come, too?"

Betty turned the question to me. "What do you say? You want her?"

"You're not going to tell me that I'm crazy, are you?"

"No." She ran her fingers nervously through her hair. "In fact, I don't think you're crazy at all. I do think something's going on. Axel isn't acting right."

See? I had told her so. But now wasn't the time to be all high-and-mighty. "What do you mean? What happened?"

I was genuinely curious and watched as Cordelia nibbled her bottom lip before answering. "He was acting funny."

"Would you care to elaborate? A lot of people can act funny," I countered.

"All right." Cordelia exhaled like she had to steel herself. "Larkin told me that Axel, or Adam, or whoever he is, has been asking a lot of questions—things that he should already know about the clan. And not only that, but I saw him this week and he asked if I was going into work and then pointed to the hotel. I reminded him that I worked at Magical Wishes, and he acted like he'd momentarily forgot. Pepper, I left the hotel ages ago, you know that. Axel would've remembered. It wasn't right and he wasn't joking. He was completely serious when he thought that I was walking to the hotel."

"He's being careless," Betty said. "Very careless. If Adam finds himself pushed into a corner, he'll pounce. No doubt about that."

My mind was whirling. Why would Adam have made such obvious mistakes? He'd been gone a long time, and I assumed that he had Axel captive so that he could pry information out of him. The easiest answer, one that made the most sense, was that my husband was lying to Adam, not telling him the truth about things.

But why?

Then I had it. "Axel's trying to tell us something."

Cordelia and Betty glanced at me. "What?" my grandmother said.

"Axel purposefully fed Adam incorrect information so that he'll be found out. He wants those of us in town to know that Adam's an imposter."

Betty stroked her chin. "Makes a lot of sense. I like it. He's trying to drop clues. Wonder if he could drop one about where he is."

"That's why we're going back to the sewers, remember?" I said.

"Right. Well, I'm ready. Cordelia, you need an outfit?"

"Yes, please."

Betty fixed my cousin up with her own commando-style getup in no time. The three of us stood in the living room, staring at one another. It was a somber moment. My husband was out there, somewhere, and only a few of us knew about it. We had to find him because at some point, his time would run out.

"Should we pray?" Betty said. I nodded. We took hands and my grandmother started. "Lord, we ask that you guide us in the sewers tonight, and that if there is a man hurting inside those tunnels, that you help us to find him. Lord, he needs hope and is missing his family. His family misses and needs him, too. We ask that if you see fit, that you reunite them. Oh, and we also ask that you give the person who is responsible for all this hurt a real kick in the behind, because he deserves it, too."

A small laugh blasted from Cordelia. She quickly got it under control as Betty finished up.

After we all said, "Amen," it was time to go on a hunt. This time, I wasn't coming back without my husband.

CHAPTER 18

It was my third time in the sewer and hopefully my last. It didn't smell as bad as I remembered. It was like the more I was down in the tunnels, the less horrible the stench seemed.

Strange, right?

But anyway, Cordelia, Betty and I were slowly making our way through the sludgy water.

I had decided that we needed to head more to the right, toward the center of town. It was the one direction that I'd been going in when the alligator found me, and it was also in that direction that the alligator suit had been found. So to me, that meant something was going on in that direction, something that needed to be unearthed.

We had only been walking a few minutes when a low growl caught my attention. I came to a halt. "Did y'all hear that?"

"I did," Cordelia said.

Betty nodded. "Sounded like it was coming from that direction."

She pointed to an area that was illuminated by a floating light ball, an area where somehow it appeared that weeds had sprouted down beneath the earth, slinking through cracks in the pipes. Vegetation hung like curtains from the top of the tunnel. How was that even possible? There wasn't sunlight down there. How could plants be growing?

They couldn't unless it had been placed there by someone bound and determined to keep us out of an area—someone like Adam.

I whispered to Betty as we ventured ever so cautiously, practically on our tiptoes, forward. "Do you think somehow Gilda Goldenheart is involved?"

She shrugged. "I don't know. Not purposefully, I'm sure. But she's not usually one to hold to rules very closely. She tends not to care very much, which was why I found it strange that she wouldn't give you the blueprints. Who cares about blueprints?"

"I care about y'all talking so much," Cordelia snipped. "Y'all are loud enough to wake the dead—or an alligator."

"We're using our inside voices," Betty griped.

"You sound like you learned how to whisper in the middle of a hailstorm."

"You're just jealous that you don't know as much about our town as I do," Betty informed my cousin.

Cordelia rolled her eyes. "Yeah, that's it. I'm jealous. I'm not at all worried about my own safety. I'm totally envious that you know how Gilda Goldenheart does busine—"

A growl rumbled through the tunnels, vibrating all the way through my chest.

The three of us stopped. "What was that?" I asked.

"Sounded like Godzilla," Betty replied.

"It's not Godzilla," Cordelia said through gritted teeth. "Can we please not jump off the deep end and into a bottomless ocean?"

Betty lifted her chin. "I'm only being realistic. Fine. It was a T. rex instead."

The growl came again, this time louder, stronger.

It shook the walls. Heck, even the weird weeds that apparently only grew in extreme darkness shivered.

"I think our gator is that way," I said, forcing my feet forward. They didn't want to go, but I wasn't going to give them any choice in the matter. I glanced over my shoulder to make sure that my family was with me, but they hadn't moved. "Are y'all coming?" I ground out.

Betty had gone pale as a plate, and Cordelia's mouth was twisted into such a fierce grimace, I didn't know if it would ever right itself. I really hoped it did because if she wound up getting married to Larkin or anyone else, her bridal pictures would be horrific.

"Y-yes, we're coming." Betty hooked her arm through Cordelia's and yanked. "Aren't we, Cordelia?"

"Um, yeah. I'll follow behind y'all."

I curled my hands into fists. "If y'all are too scared to come, fine. But I'm going. I've got to know what's happened to Axel."

The grimace melted off Cordelia's face. "I'm coming. We're going to find Axel and get to the bottom of this. Even if we do get eaten."

Oh, Lawd. "We're not going to be eaten. Now, let's go."

The three of us headed into the depths of the tunnels. My hackles were up as worry wormed its way to my core. Betty had been right in her assessment that the roar resembled a dinosaur's. It was loud, hair-raising, even.

As we neared, a low rumble filled the tunnel. It had a rhythm to it, almost like something was moving back and forth, back and forth.

"Is that alligator sawing logs?" Betty said, a euphemism for snoring.

Baffled, I replied, "It sure does sound like it."

"Maybe we can catch it unaware and find Axel," Cordelia replied.

I could only hope.

The tunnel up ahead was draped in those seaweedy-looking vines. I just…couldn't cope with the underground vegetation. Like, why was something growing down here? Just to make me more nervous? Just to frustrate me and add to my anxiety? It didn't make sense.

We all stopped outside the threshold that the creeping vines created.

"You first, girls," Betty whispered. "I'll bring up the rear."

"How about you go ahead?" Cordelia said. "You know, age before beauty."

Betty frowned. She did not like being called old. "Oh no, I insist that you push on ahead. You're the adventurous one of us, Cordelia."

"Not like you," my cousin argued.

Tired of their bickering, I was about to charge on ahead when I noticed something. The sawing sound had stopped.

"Shh. It's not going anymore."

"Probably because of your cousin," Betty said.

"Quiet," I snarled. "I'll look."

I plucked one of the light orbs from the air and headed through the weeds. One of them slid over my back as I edged forward, and the stupid thing tickled my neck. It took everything I had not to scream bloody murder.

But anyway, I walked slowly into the tunnel. It was dim, somehow seeming darker than the others. I noticed first off what looked like a pile of branches. They were smashed down as if someone or something had been lying on them.

Oh, crap. We'd found the alligator's bed. But where was the creature?

That was when a growl caught my attention. There, off in the shadows, something stepped forward.

The alligator!

It lunged for me, jaws clacking as they came down to bite my arm or leg off. I was sure the alligator wouldn't be picky about which part of me it devoured. It would take whatever appendage it could get.

Scared out of my mind, I did the only thing I could think—I threw magic on the beast. It was a halting spell and should have stopped it in its tracks.

But my magic just splashed off it, dissolving onto the floor.

"Run," I screamed.

Betty and Cordelia didn't have to be asked twice.

We raced through the sewers. Betty must've magicked her legs because they were pumping something fierce as she motored like a boat through the corridors.

Cordelia glanced back. "It's gaining on us."

I wasn't going to look over my shoulder to make sure she was right. In a horror movie, every time some dumb too-stupid-to-be-alive girl glanced back, she fell and was picked off by the killer. It was that simple, so I wasn't going to be that stupid, thank you very much.

I shouted back to my cousin, "I already tried magic. It didn't work."

"Maybe you didn't use the right spell."

As I could hear the alligator panting behind me, I wasn't going to argue what spell I used. So instead I called out, "You try."

She gave a quick look back, pointed her finger and aimed. I heard the spell hit the creature. It sounded like water splashing on a body. And yes, I dared to look behind me. The alligator roared and charged even faster.

What was going on?

"My spell didn't work," Cordelia cried.

"That's what I was saying. It's not affected by magic."

Betty, who had slowed (I suppose so that she could remain with us peasants), shouted back, "Magic not working on the creature? I don't believe it."

"Then you try," I said.

"Will do."

Betty opened her hand, and a blue swirling egg of power formed. Literally, it looked like an Easter egg, one that a child dipped in several colors of dye in order to get a deep patchy blue. If I hadn't been afraid for my life, I might've admired just how pretty it was.

But as it was, you know, there was the whole fearful-of-dying thing that was taking up most of my thoughts.

"This will stop an elephant," Betty yelled before sending the ball zooming down the tunnel straight at me.

Straight. At. Me. The ball was coming for me. If it hit, then I'd blow up or fall down and the alligator would literally eat me alive.

Or I'd explode into a thousand smithereens. Neither were good predictions for my future.

I veered to the left just as the egg sailed past. I glanced back just as a huge *splat* filled the corridor.

The sewer exploded in light. It also exploded in force. I was thrown forward, the light so blinding that I couldn't see. Everything became a jumbled mess. I didn't know where Cordelia and Betty were, or if the gator had been stopped.

I fell hard on my knees in the stinky water. It took a minute to feel right as a wave of nausea overcame me. *What did you cast, Betty?*

I shook off the feeling and started to get up just as a low growl came from behind me. A quick glance over my shoulder told me that the alligator was momentarily stopped by the blinding light, but it wasn't hurt or harmed in any shape or form.

Magic simply didn't affect it. At all. It was immune.

How was that possible?

Betty and Cordelia were nowhere to be seen, which I took to mean that they (since they weren't as close to ground zero as I had been) had been able to get farther down the tunnels and had probably reached safety at that point. At least, I hoped that they had.

The alligator's tail swished back and forth, and I couldn't help but to be reminded of a cat right before it pounced on its prey.

"Good alligator," I said. "I'm not going to hurt you. I just want to know what happened to my husband, where he is." An idea came to me. Perhaps I could speak to the creature telepathically. *Can you hear me?*

But the creature didn't respond. I tried again, louder, because you know, what if it was hard of hearing? But there was still no response.

Since gators were an old species and related to dinosaurs, their brains tended to be much more primal, which was probably why I couldn't communicate with it. It was the same with birds, though they were a bit more hit-or-miss.

But I digressed. The alligator was closing in, tail swishing, jaws snapping. I threw out my hand to create a portal, something that would get me out of there, but my magic sparked and then fizzled out.

Crap. My brain was just as frazzled as my magic. I was in fight-or-flight and all my energy was focused on the gator instead, which meant that my magic wasn't wanting to form something as technical as a portal.

I could try to run again, but the gator would only catch up to me then. Just as I was weighing my options, a hand reached down from the ceiling.

"Come on. Let me help you."

I glanced up to see Ellen. She'd uncovered a manhole and was literally offering me a hand.

I grabbed her arm as the gator closed in and she pulled me up and away from the jaws of death.

CHAPTER 19

"Thank you," I gushed when I was safely aboveground.
Ellen smiled. "You're welcome."

I was lying on my back, staring up at the sky. My legs had been so weak that when I attempted to stand, they'd given out. So I was inhaling and exhaling, trying to calm my heart that was pumping like crazy.

"I'm so glad you were here," I said to her. "If you hadn't been, I don't know what would've happened."

Ellen played with one of the two ropes of braids that ran over each of her shoulders. "You're welcome."

As soon as I'd laid down, I'd texted Cordelia to find out where she and Betty were. They'd made it back to our entry point and were just leaving. I told them that I was okay and would catch up with them a bit later, making sure that she knew Betty's magic hadn't worked on the alligator, either. I'd left out the part that it had almost gotten me killed. Why make people feel bad if they didn't need to?

As I stared at the stars, my heart was beginning to slow and I sat up, feeling pretty good.

Ellen was still playing with her hair, and she smiled. "Better?"

"Much." I paused. "I called you the other day and left a message."

"Right," she replied, eyes widening. "Sorry. I meant to call you back, but by the time I got the message it was late. I'd left my phone at home."

So that explained why I'd heard it ringing in her house.

I stretched my arms over my head. "What are the chances that you would be out at night twice, both on occasions when I've been in the sewer, being pursued by an alligator?"

"Yeah, I know. Totally random, right?"

But what if it wasn't random at all? What if Ellen was here for a reason? It just didn't make sense. It couldn't have been coincidence that she happened to show up in Magnolia Cove near the sewers the two nights that I'd gone schlepping in the tunnels.

What was up?

I smiled at her, doing my best to make the look on my face sincere. I was pretty sure if Axel had been here, he would've told me that my face looked like I was suffering from constipation.

Goodness, how I missed him.

If I let myself think about his absence too much, an ache throbbed in my heart. It was soul crushing that Adam had done something with him. I'd become good at focusing on the fact that we needed to find Axel, but if I let myself think about him too long, I'd break down. I'd find the nearest bed, pull the covers over my head and never resurface.

I knew that he ached for me, too.

But back to the ever-so-suspicious Ellen and her ability to appear at the right place at the right time. In fact, the more I thought about it, the more frustrated I became at her presence. It wasn't natural.

So I bit out, "What are you doing here?"

She jerked back, surprised by the venom in my voice. "I'm on my way home from my aunt's."

"But you could take several different paths to enter the Cobweb Forest. Why choose this one?"

"It's the path I like."

I narrowed my eyes. Like, I could even feel my brows pinching in a really witchy manner. "But don't you think it's strange that you happen to be here, and you didn't seem all that surprised earlier to find out about the alligator. That's weird, don't you think? Not a common occurrence in a town. In fact, the sheriff took some of us down into the depths of the tunnels just yesterday and we didn't find hide nor hair of the gator. Only an alligator suit. Don't you think that's out of the ordinary?"

She wiped sweat from her brow. Oh, I had her. But what was it that I'd caught Ellen in? A lie? A cover-up?

The young woman smiled widely, seeming to toss aside her worry like a pair of dirty panties. "I like this walk, that's all. Sometimes there are coincidences in life, and I don't know, I've encountered strange animals before. So I guess the gator didn't really surprise me."

Like Ross had said, Ellen used to be a beast hunter. "And you've seen a lot of creatures?"

"Yes," she explained. "I used to travel a lot. They have all kinds of rare beasts in Europe. You wouldn't believe what you'd find in the deep forests there—gremlins and griffins, sprites and succubae—all sorts of strange and wonderful creatures."

I didn't think succubae were particularly wonderful, but to each his own. "And alligators? Any of those?"

"Er, no, but like I said, you've seen one magical creature, you've seen them all."

"I didn't say the alligator was magical."

Ellen laughed uncomfortably. "I mean, I guess that I only assumed. You know, because it's in a sewer and all. Random," she said jokingly.

But I didn't laugh. Ellen's story reeked and not of onions. This was a worse smell than that of the bodily type. She was hiding something. But it was obvious that I wasn't going to get any answers from her, not unless I put her feet to an actual fire and forced them out.

But I wasn't that sort of witch. There were other ways to uncover the truth, as I'd discovered in my years in Magnolia Cove. You know, like spying on people and following them—that sort of thing.

So I decided right then and there to find out exactly what Ellen was hiding, because deep down, I had the sinking feeling that she and Ross were working with Adam.

And I planned to prove it.

∽

I LEFT Ellen and walked home. I was tired of using magic, and besides, I needed to think. There was a lot that my mind had to shuffle through.

First, Ellen knew something about the alligator and had a connection to Adam. I mean, most likely she did. It made perfect sense.

It was as if Ellen was stationed near the sewers to make sure that either no one got in (she was terrible at that job, if that was the case) or for another reason. Perhaps she was protecting the alligator or making sure it didn't harm anyone.

That seemed the most likely scenario. She was trying to keep people safe.

But if that was the case, wouldn't she have been *in* the tunnels to do that? It appeared the wiser of the two choices.

Okay, so she wasn't there to keep anyone safe. She was there for another reason—to keep anyone from going down into the sewer. There were several points of entry, and the one that I'd escaped from tonight had been different from the one the other night.

So she was roaming, looking, searching. She had experience with creatures, as she'd said, so perhaps Adam hired her to make sure no one got near the alligator. Obviously he did that to keep his secret safe.

When I did discover his secret, Adam planted the gator suit in the tunnels. As if I was stupid enough to believe that was what I'd seen. Come on.

So...they were working together, which meant that we (my family and me) needed to find a way to ferret out the truth. I would go to Betty with my thoughts, that the three were in cahoots, and like always, we'd figure out a way to get to the bottom of things and find my husband.

A rustle in the leaves caught my attention, making my thoughts drift back to earlier in the day when I'd encountered the bird.

What a strange conversation that had been. The little chirper had said not to hurt him, as if the bird was intimately acquainted with the alligator.

I nearly chuckled at that. Impossible. The bird couldn't know the alligator. How would it? Alligators didn't hang out with birds. They weren't friends. Okay, maybe there were those birds in Africa that ate the funk from crocodiles' teeth. Total exception. But the creature in the sewer wasn't a croc and the bird I saw wasn't from Africa, so that didn't count.

But still...the bird's words nagged at me. There was something deeper there, something that I wasn't understanding.

Perhaps I needed to wrap my brain around this differently.

What if the bird did know the alligator, and what if, when the bird called it a *him*, it really did mean him. It spoke as if the alligator was more than simply a sluggish primordial brain, as if there was intelligence there.

Also, the bird had said that I knew him, too.

And then, very slowly, I started to realize what the bird was trying to tell me. I also realized the depths of Adam's evilness. Originally I'd simply believed that Adam was hiding Axel away, that he was keeping him locked somewhere.

Oh, he was keeping him locked away, but his sadistic devilry delved much deeper than simply putting my husband in a cage.

No, Adam had to make sure that no one would find Axel. He had to have assurances that my husband's true identity wouldn't be discovered.

The one way to do that was to make sure that Axel didn't look like Axel.

Rage like lava flowed through my veins as I realized what Adam had done. He'd gone too far, way too far. He had dived down to a place that was unforgivable.

When I told Betty, she'd agree with me. Now we had a brand-new problem. We knew where Axel was; we just had to figure out how to save him. I prayed that she had a spell for that, because I had a feeling that Adam would've made it nearly impossible to break the magic without his help.

That was the sort of jerk he was.

For Axel had been right under our noses this entire time. The alligator wasn't guarding him. He *was* the alligator.

And it was time to set him free.

CHAPTER 20

"The alligator is Axel," I said to Betty and Cordelia when I got to the house a few minutes later.

Cordelia hugged me with relief; then she glared at me. "Have you lost your mind?"

"No, I haven't. Let me tell you what happened."

While Betty smoked her pipe and Cordelia changed out of her black clothes, I explained about the bird, about Ellen, about the strangeness that I'd been feeling and how the only thing that made sense was what I was theorizing.

"It's logical," I practically pleaded to Betty. "Isn't it? We haven't been able to find Axel, but we've found an alligator, one that can't be harmed by magic. It must be part of the spell that Adam has put on him. Don't you think?"

I waited with bated breath while Betty thought about what I'd said. Even if she did believe that I was crazy, I'd probably just go ahead and search for a spell to release Axel on my own. Not that I'd be able to find it, mind you. More than likely the best I'd come up with was conjuring a bologna sandwich for him to eat. This was why I needed Betty.

"Well?" I prodded my grandmother.

She pulled on her pipe and dropped her head back, releasing a stream of smoke that curled into a doughnut. "I did think there was something strange about the fact that the creature wasn't touched by power. It could only mean that something magical was going on with it."

"Like what?" Amelia asked, entering with a very awake Gizzy.

She placed the baby in my arms, and Gizzy gurgled and smiled, happy to see me. I nestled my head to hers, also relieved to see my daughter. I'd missed her so much that it felt like my heart was going to pop.

"What could be happening with the creature?" Betty said, in response to Amelia's question. "It could be spelled, was what I thought, or it could have been created from magic. Sometimes things that are created from magic can't be affected by it."

"Aurora's affected by magic," I countered. "And she was created by it."

Aurora was a golem that I'd made to keep the ogre in my backyard, Grumpy, company.

"That's true," Betty agreed. "But there are some exceptions to that, exceptions where a being made from magic can be hit right in the gullet with a spell and it will dissolve at its feet."

"At the gullet's feet?" Cordelia asked sarcastically.

"You know what I mean," Betty snipped.

"I'm so tempted to say that I don't."

My grandmother rolled her eyes. "If you'd like to be serious, I'll tell you other times when I've seen curses like this."

I shot Cordelia a look. "Let's be serious."

"I am serious. I was only asking about the gullet. It was a perfectly logical question with the way that Betty phrased her sentence."

To Betty I said, "I think you can go on."

"Fine. The one and most important time when I saw something like this, when a creature wasn't affected by magic, happened because of a curse."

Everyone was silent. After a few seconds it was me who spoke, though I had to pull Gizzy's fist from my mouth to do so. "A curse? Are you suggesting that Adam cursed Axel?"

"Why wouldn't he have? He hates his brother. It would be a wonderful way to get back at him, don't you think, as it would ensure that Axel wouldn't be able to break the spell unless Adam either told someone how to do it, or broke the magic himself. It would be," she said dramatically, "the perfect revenge."

It took a moment to digest her words. Axel, cursed? Forced to live as an alligator?

"Or he could just be enchanted," Betty quickly added. "Turned into an alligator and true love's kiss will break the spell."

"I'm not kissing that gator," I said. "It'll tear my lips off."

"That's a problem," Amelia added. "Wow. This is like that saying about how you can put lipstick on a pig, but it's still a pig."

"No, it isn't," I replied. "It's nothing like that."

"Well," she whimpered, feelings hurt, "it might be."

"We need to remain on task." I handed Gizzy back to Amelia, clasped my hands behind my back and started pacing. "Whether he's cursed or enchanted, we've got to figure it out and release him. But how are we going to do that? Magic doesn't work on the creature, so we can't trap him in a bubble or anything."

"Can you speak to it?" Cordelia asked.

I shook my head. "Tried, but no go. The primal brain of the alligator is dominant. I can't find anything in there except that, and it was a blank slate."

"Hmm," Betty murmured. "This is quite the conundrum."

"I would say so," Amelia said. "If magic doesn't work, it's like there are only two options—either build a super heavy trap or throw a net on the beast and jump atop it pretending to be an alligator hunter, or get Adam to tell you what the secret is."

All gazes turned to Amelia. "What did you say?" I asked.

She shrugged. "Get Adam to tell you. You know, get him good and drunk. Wear something sexy. Maybe he'll spill the beans."

The truth serum had been such a fiasco that I hadn't considered trying to get more information out of him. But plying him with drink could work. Still, my skin crawled at the thought of him touching me. There was just something about it that made me want to hurl.

Betty walked up and smacked my arm. "Looks like you're gonna have to take one for the team, kid."

I didn't like the sound of that. My grandmother made it seem like I was about to sacrifice myself for the greater good. Well, that was what was about to happen, wasn't it?

"Oh, there's something else I haven't told you. It's about a couple named Ellen and Ross. I think they're working with Adam. I keep finding Ellen near the sewers whenever I leave."

"Could be stationed there as a protector," Betty mused. "But the good thing is, she's not in your house, so you will be free to drag whatever information out of Adam you need, any way possible."

Mischief glinted in her eyes, making bile surge up the back of my throat. "For the record, isn't there another way that we can do this? You know, one where I don't have to talk to Adam or get close to him? Spend time with the man?"

"No," Betty informed me. "But if it makes you feel better, we'll be outside to make sure that nothing goes wrong, that he doesn't wise up to what you're doing and hurt you."

"That actually doesn't make me feel much better. What would make me feel better is if I didn't have to do this at all."

Cordelia took my arm. "We'll help you. We've got time to come up with a script for you to follow. You can't do it tonight, anyway. But by tomorrow, we'll have the whole thing sorted out."

"Oh," Amelia said happily, "there's a section in my wedding book about this. In the back, it's about the wedding night."

I really wanted to hurl.

"Let me get it." She put Gizzy down and clapped her hands. The book hovered in the air, and my cousin pointed to it with one long finger. The pages flipped and stopped. "Here we are. How to have the perfect wedding night. The first thing you need, Pepper, is a negligee."

I gave her a frosty look. "I'm not wearing a negligee for Adam."

She waved away my concern. "Don't worry, you're not going to take it off."

"How can you be so sure?" I mean, really, how could she? Amelia didn't know what was going to happen at my house. "You can't be so confident."

"Yes, I can, because you're going to have a bottle of champagne that you drink and also cake that you eat and all that sugar from both will make him really tired. So you don't have to get him drunk at all. Just make him snoozy."

Oh my gosh, she was a genius. Eating sugar always made Axel tired.

So tired that right after he ever ate a big dessert, he always took a nap. If sweets did that to him, they would do the same to Adam.

"And while he's so fatigued," Betty said, "you'll use a small coaxing spell to get information out of him."

Amelia smiled. "He'll be so out of it that he won't know what he's saying."

My jaw dropped. This might have been the most brilliant. Plan. Ever. I couldn't believe it. The sugar would make him exhausted and with a little magic—not so much that he would feel it—Adam might just spill all the tea in China.

Yes! This was such a good plan I could have kissed all of them. But first we had to put it into action.

"Let's go through all the details," I said.

Cordelia snapped her fingers. "You say that you want to celebrate because Gizzy's turning six months old."

"She's already done that," I said.

She quirked a brow. "But did you celebrate it?"

"Good point." Because we hadn't celebrated, but Adam wouldn't know or care about that. "I can make that work."

"Then you get him to eat as much cake as possible," Amelia said. "The negligee will help."

"Yeah, tell him that if he isn't a good boy, then he doesn't get to see you out of it," Betty said.

Ugh. Vomit nearly spouted from my mouth. Disgusting. "Okay, so I'll tell him that and force him to drink champagne."

"By the time he's had a slice of cake and a drink, he'll be tired," Amelia said proudly.

"How do you know?" I asked.

"Because I'm going to make heart-stopping sugar cake."

"What?" I'd never heard of this recipe. "What's that?"

"It's a cake I considered serving for my wedding, but it's so sugary that folks will get tired too fast. They'd fall to sleep on the dance floor. So it's a no go."

That sounded bad. "And you're sure this won't happen to Adam."

Amelia nodded enthusiastically. Finally, she was getting to use her wedding book for something other than her own nuptials. "The key is not to serve him too much. Just enough and he'll be tired and then the coaxing, and you'll get the information you want."

"Betty?" I asked, wanting to know her opinion.

"He's a rough and tough criminal doing a good job of disguising himself as his brother. We have to be sneaky with someone like him, or else he'll figure out what we're doing, and the whole thing will be off. I think Amelia's plan is the best one we've got. Get him so relaxed that he won't even know what he's saying, and we've found our means to locating your husband. Just be careful. That's all I ask."

Be careful. That was at the top of my priority list. I didn't want to wind up dead because Adam sniffed out that I knew his true identity.

This could go one of two ways—it could either be an amazing success or I'd fail miserably. Adam would discover that I knew the truth, and he'd do everything in his power to destroy me.

The only things keeping me from freaking out were that I had to find my husband and that my family would be waiting in the wings, ready to help.

"I can do it," I said proudly. "But who's going to watch Gizzy?"

Betty winked. "Leave that to me."

CHAPTER 21

Leave that to me consisted of Shoo, Sherman and Larkin watching Gizzy. I trusted Larkin and Sherman with her. Shoo was the wild card in the bunch. But since he was with two responsible men, I figured nothing could go wrong.

Right?

Famous last words, I know.

But anyhow, it was the next night and we were ready. Cordelia had created a beautiful negligee for me and had also made a black silk robe to wear over it. Amelia had built the heart-stopping sugar cake, which was a red velvet sponge with cream cheese icing. I really, really, wanted to eat the entire thing, but then I'd fall asleep and our plan would be null and void.

Betty stationed everyone outside the house, so that all I had to do was stay inside and wait for Adam.

By myself because Mattie was out hunting.

So that was what I did.

Everything was ready. I had the cake and champagne sitting on a table. There was no dinner. That was the clincher. I would tell Adam that we'd eat after celebrating. That's what the sexy clothing was for—to distract and assist in him not wanting a huge steak.

After what seemed like forever, the front door finally opened. Heat flushed my cheeks I was so nervous. I willed the crimson that I knew stained my flesh away, and I rose to greet Adam.

"Surprise," I said, presenting the glass platter that held the cake.

His eyes flared. "What's this?"

"This," I said coyly, "is that we're celebrating Gizzy's six-month birthday." He looked doubtful, so I quickly added, "Just the two of us. All alone."

"Oh." His eyes widened in realization. "I like this idea."

He moved to place a hand on my waist, and I demurely slid away. "Let me get us some cake and champagne, and then we can have some fun."

The corners of his eyes tightened and I sensed that Adam was on to me, so I rolled onto my tip toes and pecked his cheek.

His eyes softened, and I moved to the kitchen to cut the cake. "So, how was work?"

"Oh, you know, nothing exciting," he said vacantly.

"I thought your work was always exciting."

"Not today it wasn't," he replied gruffly.

Axel would never have been that gruff with me. Adam needed to work harder if he was going to attempt to step into my husband's shoes.

But I wasn't going to let him bring me down, because I had a bigger agenda. So I sliced two pieces of cake (both huge, though I didn't plan to eat any more than a nibble) and grabbed the bottle of champagne.

I turned around to find him standing directly behind me. Shocked, the bottle slipped from my hands, but Adam caught it easily.

"Did I scare you?" he asked in a husky voice.

"Oh, no. Not at all. I just…didn't expect you to be so close."

He placed the bottle on the table behind me, and his fingers trailed over the collar of the robe. "I like this material. I'd like it more if it was on the floor."

I laughed nervously. "All in good time." Then I felt behind me for a plate, found it and shoved it into his stomach. "Cake first."

His brows pinched together. "I'm not really in the mood for sweets."

"You don't want to celebrate our daughter's half birthday?" I said in a mocking tone. "You must not be her father."

The words slipped out before I could stop them. Adam's brow pinch became a full-on scowl, but then his expression relaxed.

"Ha ha," he replied. "Very funny."

Before he could say another word, I grabbed the champagne and thrust it into his open hand. "Here. Pop this cork."

He grunted his resistance, but in the end did as I said. I made a big show as the cork rocketed across the room, clapping my hands and acting all overexcited and dramatic. It was a wonder that Adam didn't suspect something strange right then and there, but he didn't. In fact, he was smiling.

Good. As long as I kept him focused, everything would go as planned.

But I didn't count on my family.

"What's that?" Adam asked, his head swiveling toward the window.

Fear immediately jetted down my spine. "What's what?"

"I thought that I saw a light." He edged to the pane. "Out there."

Crap. Someone must've shone their flashlight. "I'm sure it was nothing. Come on. Let's have some champagne and cake, celebrate."

"No," he said gruffly. "I know that I saw it. I'm going out to check."

"I'll go with you."

"You stay here," he commanded.

Since when did I listen to anyone? I hadn't before and I wasn't about to start now.

While Adam headed out the back door, I sprinted out the front and whispered to whoever could hear me, "Can the flashlight."

"It's Amelia," Betty whispered back.

Good grief! Did they *want* to be discovered? "Stop talking," I hissed before racing back inside.

When I got there, Adam was striding in. He raked his hair from his face, and in that moment, he looked so much like Axel I was almost beginning to doubt myself.

Almost.

"It wasn't anything," he said.

I exhaled a low sigh of relief. Thank goodness he hadn't heard or seen anyone. Time to get back to business. I poured two flutes full of champagne and handed one to him.

"Ready for dessert?"

"I'm ready for you," he growled, pawing at me.

I tittered and managed to escape his grasp. "Ah, ah. Not until we've had cake. We've got to celebrate, remember?"

"How could I forget?" He took the plate that I handed him, and we sat at the table. Adam dug his fork right in. He scooped a bite into his mouth and moaned. "This is amazing."

"I'm so glad that you like it."

Meanwhile, I was pushing the food along on my plate, praying that he didn't notice that I wasn't eating like he was.

"You're not eating."

"Oh, well, I just took a bite and I'm trying to finish chewing it. See?" I made a big deal of munching on my tongue. "So good. Wow. We should have this every day."

He stared at my full plate. "I'm not going to eat another bite until I see you have one."

Oh, crap. This guy was good. First, he'd thrown me off my game so that I wound up eating the truth serum that was intended for him, and now here I was trying not to eat the cake that would make me tired and pliable. But here sat Adam once again, making sure that I did exactly the opposite of what I wanted.

I really despised him. Like, really.

"Here." He took my fork from my hand and scraped off a huge bite. "Eat this. It's so good. Just a little won't make you gain weight."

Oh, he knew all the tricks, all the tools to get me to do what he wanted. I couldn't exactly say no, now could I? If I didn't eat, then that would look suspicious. If I did eat, then I'd get tired, too. But maybe there would be enough time to coerce info out of him before I conked out.

It was a risk that I had no choice but to take. So I opened my mouth and let Adam feed me a huge wedge of heart-stopping sugar cake while I prayed that it didn't make me immediately keel over from fatigue.

As soon as the creamy frosting hit my mouth, I instantly wanted more. There was something about it that I couldn't put my finger on— the richness of the red velvet, the creaminess of the frosting, combined with all the sugar that had been used to create the sponge made it absolutely addicting and only with one bite.

"So good," I murmured.

He took his own bite. "Yes, it is. Here, have another."

My hackles rose. I couldn't keep letting him feed me. "No, no. I want to go slow."

"I insist." He paid no attention to my protests as he cut off another hunk and shoved it in my mouth. "There you go. Eat up. There's plenty for both of us."

Oh, jeez, that was good. But I was beginning to feel it. My lids were getting heavy, and I was already stifling a yawn. If I was going to keep my wits about me, I had to turn this conversation around to benefit me.

So I cut off a hunk of cake from my own plate and shoved it in Adam's face. "Here, let me feed you."

"Don't mind if I do." After he ate the cake, I handed him the champagne. "Be sure to wash it down." He tossed his head back, and every last drop in the glass slid down his throat. "Let me get you more."

I kept Adam so busy feeding and watering him that he didn't have time to shovel any more cake in my face. After about ten minutes, he was getting tired. His eyelids were hoods, and his jaw was becoming slack.

Now it was time for the spell. "Let me get these plates out of our way."

I rose and walked past Adam as he feebly pawed at me. As I washed the dishes up, I was inwardly working the spell to coax him, summoning my magic. For some reason, coaxing worked best with black pepper, perhaps because of its abilities to make one sneeze. So I sprinkled a little into my palm and headed back to the table.

All I had to do was sprinkle the grains of pepper onto Adam's head. It was the last piece of the spell, and then I could ask him whatever I wanted.

My heart leaped with excitement. In only a few moments I would know how to free Axel from whatever curse or enchantment that Adam had put him under.

I sprinkled the grains on top of his head without Adam noticing, thank goodness, and then I sat back across from him. He glanced over, his eyes glazy.

"I'm suddenly so tired," he said, punctuating his words with a yawn at the end.

"I know. I'm sorry, but I need help."

"I can't help you," he said lazily.

He didn't even know what I was asking, but the sly smile on his face made me think that he was joking. Gosh, Adam was so much like Axel that it was eerie. "There's a spell, or an enchantment," I told him gently. "I need to know about it."

His head bobbed to the shoulder closest to me. "It can't be broken."

Wow, he knew exactly what I was talking about! Adam was happily giving me all the information that I needed. Thank goodness. But I didn't like that whole part that it couldn't be broken. That didn't sound good.

"What can't be broken?" I prodded.

"The curse." His gaze swiveled to land directly on me. The weight of his stare made the hairs on the back of my head soldier to attention. "It's the dark curse of a twin."

He was the twin and it was a dark curse because of him. That was what he meant, right? But what did that even mean? I needed more info.

"But there must be a way to break it," I said.

The low rumble of a laugh began in his chest until it spewed from his mouth. "There is no cure. There's no way to stop it. It's done and nothing you can do will end what's been set in motion."

With that, his head dropped to his chest and Adam fell asleep.

CHAPTER 22

When he was totally passed out, I gathered my family and headed back to Betty's. There, we found Shoo standing on one foot while balancing a ball on his nose.

Gizzy was staring up at him and laughing.

"Food coming through," Sherman called from the kitchen. He charged into the living room with Larkin behind him.

"You can't feed her roast chicken," Larkin snapped.

Sherman shook his head. "She can eat roast chicken. She's got teeth."

Larkin pointed to the poultry leg on the plate Sherman was carrying. "She can't eat it like that. It's got to be in smaller bites. You'll choke her."

Sherman approached me. He held the plate proudly. "Can I, or can I not feed this to Gizzy."

"You cannot," I said.

Larkin took the plate from Sherman. "As I said. It's got to be in smaller bites." He rolled his eyes at me. "Don't worry, I'll fix it."

I had to admit that between the three of them, they had the situation with the *one* six-month-old under control.

While they were fussing with Gizzy, I rounded up the women and got to business. "Adam told me that it's the curse of a twin. Betty, have you ever heard of anything like that?"

She rubbed her chin in thought. "Seems to me what he's saying is that the curse is bonded to him, that it's tethered between them."

"How do you break something like that?" Amelia asked, all doe-eyed and full of worry.

"You need them both in the same place at the same time," Betty mused. "But it'll take a lot of research for me to figure out exactly what we're dealing with, here. I've never heard of one person being turned into a creature and the other human, and still the curses being tied."

Cordelia sucked her teeth. "What do you mean—you've never of one person a creature and one a human in a twin curse."

"Pepper, do you remember when your magic was tied to Rufus's?" Betty asked.

How could I forget? When Rufus was still evil, he'd tethered himself to me. It was a horrible feeling. "Of course I remember."

"You were both human," Betty said. "Axel, as we know, is a creature. It makes more sense that since he's a creature, that Adam would be one, too. It's the twin part of the curse."

"Oh, I get it," Amelia said. "They should either both be alligators or both be humans."

"Perhaps not an alligator, but another animal," Betty clarified. "But in order to know how to break such a curse, we first have to know more about it. I'll have to do some research. That will take time, Pepper. I don't expect to have the answers tomorrow."

"I'll lend a hand," Cordelia said. "I'm not letting my cousin-in-law remain an alligator any longer than he has to."

My heart throbbed with thanks.

"I'll help, too," Amelia added. "Axel's a good man, and he doesn't deserve to be hurt by Adam. We'll figure this out, Pepper. Don't you worry. All of us, we'll do what we can to fix this."

I gave my family a huge smile. "Thank you, all of you, for your help."

"Course," Betty proclaimed. "What else is family for?" She gave me a long look, and I could see tears pricking her eyes. But before they had a chance to spill down her cheeks, the wetness vanished.

Inwardly I chuckled. Oh, Betty. Now there was a woman who didn't like to look weak in front of anyone, not even her own family. "I'll help with finding the cure, too."

"No," Amelia said.

My brows pinched. "Why not?"

"Don't you think that you've done enough suspicious stuff? You're supposed to be fixing your store, remember?"

Oh my gosh. With Axel's disappearance I'd just about forgotten my store and the animals. I needed to get my familiar shop back in order. It was just that I'd been so distracted.

But still, what Amelia said tugged at my heartstrings. "So I can't help?"

"You can help, but you'd best keep it to a minimum," Betty said. "You don't want Adam to wise up to our plans. In order to do that, you've got to put things back to normal."

"Yeah, it seems about time for that," Cordelia said. "You should try to act like nothing's wrong."

"But…but…what about Gizzy?" I asked.

"Hmm. We don't want him getting his hands on the child and attempting something. We don't know what his ultimate plan is."

Take over Axel's life? Pretend to be his brother until he dies from old age? "His plan is to infiltrate Axel's entire existence. I still worry for our daughter. I don't want her near Adam."

"You're right," Betty agreed. "Just you, then. You've got to be a wife to him, no matter how hard it is. And you've got to pretend that he's your husband. Now, I'm not saying you've got to do anything you don't want. But while I'm studying up, we need Adam thinking everything is hunky-dory, that we're not on to him. And that means, first off, that when he wakes up tomorrow, he needs to do so in his own bed—with you beside him."

The very thought made my skin crawl. But she was right. This was a game, and we had to play it to the upmost. "Okay," I said reluctantly. "I'll do what I can. But there is a line that I'm drawing, and if he gets too touchy touchy, I'll probably conk him over the head."

Amelia laughed. "Sherman can relate to that."

They weren't married, so I could understand. But anyway, we came up with a plan that forced me to go home and leave my daughter still with Betty, and so I did.

Betty portalled me back, and Adam was where I'd left him, asleep at the table. Ugh. I really, really, didn't want to have to move him. But he needed to not recall much (or any) of our earlier conversation, so with a wiggle of my finger, I was able to lift him like a marionette.

He weighed a ton. I wasn't joking. Even though I was using magic, my finger only acted like a lever, cutting down on the weight I was lifting. Which meant I still had to burden a good part of his one hundred and eighty pounds, or however much he weighed.

But I managed to get him up and to bed. Afterward I changed my clothes and slipped in beside him, putting a pillow between us. In case he rolled over, I didn't want him touching me.

If I had to make it look like I was married to this imposter, fine. But there were still limits to how far I was going to go—and a lot of them, too.

While I lay in bed (totally wide awake because how could I sleep beside a criminal), my mind began to drift. Thoughts of Axel filled my head, about how we could often communicate telepathically.

Hold. On.

When I'd reached out to the alligator earlier, I'd only done so on the surface level. But if I dug deeper, maybe I could reach Axel.

If I was able to communicate with him, maybe he'd tell me how to break the curse that Adam had put him under.

Why hadn't I thought of this before?

I cursed myself as I climbed quietly from bed and padded back down the stairs. All right, the first thing needed for complete and utter focus was an environment conducive to concentrating.

The living room was perfect. Moonlight cut through the wooden blinds, creating ribs of light that danced across the floor. It gave enough illumination that I could see, but it wasn't distracting at all. I settled myself onto the couch and inhaled and exhaled.

It took all my focus to open up my mind, to let myself relax and my worry melt away. Finally, after several minutes I felt connected enough that I tossed out the words, fishing for his presence.

Axel? Are you there?

I waited for several long minutes, hoping that he would hear me. When there was no response, I tried again.

Axel? I'm trying to find you. I know what's going on.

This time I waited even longer before giving it one last shot. *Axel, please talk to me! I'm so worried about you.*

But by the time those last words had leaked from my head, spewing into the world, I knew it was no use. He wouldn't or, more likely, couldn't answer. The curse or enchantment that had turned him into an alligator had also bricked up his mind. He was walled in, trapped in some sort of prison. That was why I couldn't break through to the alligator when I'd attempted to speak to him earlier.

The gator's pea-sized brain was in control, and Axel had been pushed back and away.

This was disturbing news. Adam's spell was so thorough that he had succeeded in pushing Axel's mind back, replacing his very frontal thoughts with that of the beast's. It was like when Axel used to change into a werewolf. The primal side of his nature always took over, pushing Axel to the side. He had no control.

What was going on with the enchantment or curse was similar. Adam had forced Axel to disappear, replacing his consciousness with that of the gator's. Would there be long-lasting effects from it?

When Axel was a werewolf, he was never a wolf for more than one night. By the next morning he always returned to his human form. But that wasn't what was happening here. Axel was an alligator morning and night. What did being exposed to such a primordial brain do to someone long-term?

Best-case scenario, there were no long-term effects. Once we broke the spell, Axel would be Axel and we'd all rejoice as we tossed Adam into prison for the second time and threw away the key, never to let him see one slice of sunlight for the rest of his life.

Worst-case scenario...a shiver raced to my toes just thinking about it.

In the absolute worst-case scenario, we would change Axel back, but having had his human consciousness out of reach for such a long period of time would take a toll. Meaning, he would be the same man physically, but his mind would be gone, replaced with that of an alligator's for the rest of his days.

Stop. I couldn't think this way. Going down this rabbit hole wasn't good for me, and it wasn't good for Axel. I had to keep the faith.

A sharp pain stabbed my gut, and I bent over, grabbing a pillow and shoving it in my face so that Adam wouldn't hear my cry. All of this was messing with my body. My bowels were a disaster from the stress.

I couldn't let it show. Worse, I couldn't believe this way. Axel would return to us the same man that he had been before he left. There was nothing else to it. I wouldn't accept a different result.

The stomach pain ceased, and I exhaled a low breath, knowing that it was time to return to bed. But as I eased up the stairs quiet as a mouse, I couldn't shake the feeling that when we saved Axel, he wouldn't return to us the same man that he had been only a few days ago.

He would be changed, different.

But that had probably been part of Adam's plan all along.

CHAPTER 23

*I*t took all my restraint not to pour milk over Adam's head the next morning, and that was putting it kindly.

All night, I tossed and turned, thinking of the torture that Axel was going through and unable to do anything about it. I didn't like feeling powerless, but that was what I was—neutered.

So as soon as Adam was out the door (he attempted to kiss me goodbye, but I "accidentally" smacked him with a roll of paper towels), I headed over to Betty's.

But I hadn't gotten very far when I spotted Ross walking down the street.

What was he doing coming from town? Had he taken alligator watch the night before?

He and Ellen were involved with Adam. I just knew it, but it needed to be proven.

So I put on a big smile and waved. "Hey, how're you this morning?"

Ross waved back. "Good. How're you?"

"Just fine." *For someone who's searching for her husband, that is.* He gave me a casual grin, but I wasn't buying it. "I ran into Ellen the other night."

"Oh?"

"Yeah, she was on her way home from visiting her aunt. Which town did you say that she lived in, again?"

"Burnt Brook."

I rolled the words over on my tongue. "Burnt Brook. Huh. That's a nice little town. I know so many people there. What's her aunt's name?"

Ross ran his long fingers through his hair. Well, if I did say so myself, that was the universal sign for—*I'm nervous*. "Well, um, I'm sure you don't know her."

"Try me."

He chuckled and rocked back on his heels. "Sounds like you're challenging me more than you are seeing if you know the woman."

It was my turn to laugh. "I just know a lot of people, is all." Total lie. I didn't know anyone in Burnt Brook. Had never even visited the place. After all, what reason was there to leave Magnolia Cove? Except, of course, to visit other countries and see their points of interest, that was. But I kept all that to myself. "If Ellen's sick aunt is someone I know, I'd like to send her a get-well basket. Or at least a card. She may need some cheering up."

"Er, right. Well, in that case, her aunt is Gertrude Singleton."

"Shucks," I said, almost sounding too sappy to believe, "you're right. I don't know her. But I hope that Ms. Singleton gets better. It must be scary for you that Ellen's been walking home all by herself at night. You know, when you could probably meet her halfway or something."

His cheerful smile tightened. "There are things that I have to do at night, other priorities that take my time away. Trust me, Ellen is perfectly capable of taking care of herself."

"I'm sure she is," I murmured. "Oh, that reminds me. You haven't happened to see any of my animals, have you? The ones that Axel and I were looking for the day we stopped by?"

He startled. "Your animals? No. Like I said then, I don't know anything about them. Wish I did, though. And if you do find them, let me know."

"I sure will," I replied tightly.

There was a lie in his words. My question had seemed to shake Ross, worry him. He knew something about the whereabouts of my animals —but what?

He gave me a frosty goodbye. *Me.* He gave it to *me.* If anyone was going to give someone the cold shoulder, it should've been me throwing it at him, not the other way around.

But anyway, I would worry about Ross and what he was hiding later. First things first, I needed to see my family and prove what I already knew—that there was no aunt in Burnt Brooke.

I arrived at Betty's house to a frenzy. Gizzy was wailing up a storm. Amelia and Cordelia were jumping around, scratching under their armpits in an apparent attempt to look like monkeys. Betty was nowhere to be seen.

"What's going on?" I asked.

Amelia pointed to Gizzy. "She's been crying all morning and won't stop."

I rushed over and pulled Gizzy from the high chair. "Oh, my sweet baby, what's wrong?" As soon as she saw me, her tears immediately stopped and the baby plunged her face into my neck. "Did you miss me? Oh, sweet girl. I'm so sorry." I glanced up at my cousins, who were still making ridiculous faces. "Maybe it's time I took her home. She's been away too long."

"I think you're right," Amelia said, finally relaxing her posture. "Betty left too early this morning to witness Gizzy's meltdown, but I'm sure she'd agree."

The trouble was, I didn't want Gizzy near Adam. He couldn't be trusted. On the other hand, he hadn't pushed me on where she was, and he hadn't come charging into Betty's to steal her away. So…maybe Adam's ultimate goal wasn't to steal Gizzy and hide her in the mountains where no one could find her.

As long as I kept the baby near and made sure to keep her monitor on, then perhaps if Adam did try anything sneaky or surreptitious, I'd be made aware of it before he even had a chance to act.

I could also ask Mattie to sleep in Gizzy's room to keep an eye on her. My cat would do it. She adored the baby.

So it was decided. "I'll take her with me today," I told my cousins. "Betty left, you said?"

"Early this morning." Cordelia wiped down the table, which was littered with food bits. I guessed Gizzy had thrown one epic of a temper tantrum. "Said she had an idea about the curse and wanted to check it out."

Hopefully her idea would turn into a solution. I stayed with my cousins for a few more minutes before packing up Gizzy and myself and heading for Familiar Place.

My store was an empty shell except for the one kitten I'd found in the sewers. Okay, I had to do something about the shop because it looked like a ghost town.

As much as I didn't want to, and as much as I wanted to hold out that we would find my animals, I had to face facts—they weren't coming back. I wouldn't find them. It had been simple dumb luck that the kitten had crossed paths with me. At this point, the others were far away, probably living their best lives in the Cobweb Forest.

So for the first hour of my store being open (but who was going to shop in a place that had no inventory?), I perused every animal catalog that I had, eventually placing a modest order that would at least give me some variety in the shop.

I did my best not to overdo it, but I did love me some shopping, and the pictures of the puppies and kittens that were available were adorable. I wanted to buy them all. But in the end I found a way to curb my desire to buy all one hundred that were being shown and managed to only acquire five of each.

See? I was doing good.

As soon as that was done, I settled down to get to the real business at hand—Ellen's aunt. If I was going to prove that Ellen and Ross were involved with Adam, the first thing that I had to do was find out if the (mysterious) aunt that Ellen saw every day was, in fact, a real living and breathing human being.

So feeling awfully confident and a bit smug, if I did say so myself, I pulled out my phone and dialed the number for information at Burnt Brook. Now, that town wasn't magical like Magnolia Cove, but they were incorporated, which meant that they had their own police department and city hall.

Even though the world had been seduced by technology, there were still enough older folks out there to demand that their towns and cities print up the yellow and white pages so that they could find the phone number of their favorite business.

All I had to do was search for Burnt Brook's directory assistance. That number was easy enough to locate and I dialed.

The call was answered on the second ring by a woman with a ridiculously stereotypical nasal voice. "Burnt Brook directory assistance. How may I direct your call?"

"Oh, hello. My name is Pepper Reign and I'm trying to find the phone number of a woman who's an old acquaintance of my grandmother's. You see, Granny can't remember much these days"—no one tell Betty that I said that—"and she'd love to reunite with this dear, old friend of hers."

"Certainly. What's the name of the individual that you're seeking?"

"Her name's Gertrude Singleton."

"Hmm. Let me put that in." In the background I could hear the woman punching the name into her keyboard. "I'm afraid there's no one by that name here."

My heart pounded in my chest. *I knew it!* "Are you sure? My grandmother just insists that Gertrude lives in Burnt Brook."

"I'm sure. I tried spelling the name several different ways. There's no Gertrude Singleton here."

"Well, perhaps she died," I said.

"No, ma'am," the woman insisted. Then she told me information that proved my hypothesis about Ellen and Ross. "I've lived in Burnt Brook my entire life. It's a small town and not once, not ever, has there been one Singleton who resides here, and especially not a Gertrude."

I thanked the woman and hung up, quietly cheering to myself. This proved that Ellen and Ross were liars. There was no ill aunt that Ellen pretended to visit during the day. She and Ross were helping Adam with his evil plan.

Now I just had to prove it.

But how?

I had to talk to Betty. We would need to set up a way to get Ross, Ellen, Adam and Axel as the alligator all in the same place at the same time.

It was the only way to prove it. Of course, it could also help if Sheriff Rob was there. But then again, he could think that my plan was crazy, as I didn't actually have evidence that Axel was an alligator other than my own sixth sense.

Which was hardly ever wrong, if I did say so myself.

But still, this entire situation was big, which meant that I needed big help. A stab of sorrow hit me. I missed Axel. I wanted him here. He was who I looked to in times like these.

I inhaled deeply and threw back my shoulders. Well, it was my turn to save him. He'd been there for me through thick and thin and had saved me numerous times.

It was time for me to return the favor.

I dialed Betty's number, but it went straight to voice mail, which wasn't even set up, by the way. No surprise there. My grandmother found technology impossible. If technology could have spoken, it would have said the same thing about her.

Just as I was about to tuck my phone away, it rang. Betty's number flared on the screen. Great!

I answered by talking. "I have proof that Ross and Ellen are involved."

"Who?" she snipped.

I rolled my eyes. Seriously? "The people I told you about before."

"Right. Okay, great. Well, I've got some news for you."

"What is it?" My heart was beating so fast I thought it would pop out of my chest. "Spill it."

"I spent all morning going through the books at the old folks' home."

I wiggled my ear to make sure that it wasn't stopped up. "I'm sorry. What? The old folks' home? Why'd you go there?"

"Because the geriatrics in this town like to hide their books of magic. They don't believe you young people deserve to know their secrets."

"That seems awfully selfish."

"Sounds about right to me. What if you go and do something foolish with the magic, like use it against the old folks?"

I shrugged. "Well, they've already lived their lives if they're at a home. I mean, don't you think?"

Her irritation came through the phone loud and clear. "That's all you young ones care about—yourselves. If a few octogenarians die in the process, no problem."

"I'm only joking, Betty. I just think it's strange that there would be an entire library full of magical books in the basement of the nursing home, where they play bingo and make paper flowers."

"How'd you know about the paper flowers?"

I nearly scraped my fingers down my face in frustration. Could we get on with this? "I didn't. Anyway. What did you call to tell me?"

"I've found what we're looking for."

Hope leaped from my chest. "You've discovered a way to save Axel?"

I could practically hear the smile being carved onto her face. "I sure have."

CHAPTER 24

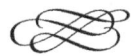

"We'll need Axel and Adam together in order to work the spell," Betty explained back at her house.

Cordelia and Amelia were there, too. Amelia's wedding book sat on the coffee table. It was so big that I swore it stared at us.

"Pepper," my grandmother said, "can you find a way to get Adam down into the sewer?"

"I'm sure he'll come if he thinks that I'm going to discover what he's done. I'll find a way."

"Excuse me." Amelia raised her hand. "This may be way off, but it seems like every time y'all come close to seeing the alligator, it chases y'all. Don't you think it would be better if you captured it and then rounded up Adam? Because the way I see it, y'all will have Adam down in the sewer with you and then the alligator will attack, Betty's wig will fall off, and y'all will be more focused on hightailing it out of there than you will be on stopping the enchantment."

"She's got a point," Cordelia said. "We need to get the alligator out of the sewer without being eaten and then get Adam and perform the spell."

"This makes things more complicated," Betty said.

I sipped from a glass of sweet tea that my grandmother had made.

Gizzy played on the floor but was eyeing my glass with want. Like any good Southern girl, her desire for tea was starting young.

I liked that.

"How does it make things more complicated?" I asked Betty.

"Because y'all will have to catch the gator while I'll be preparing the spell. Before, if we were all together in the sewer, then I'd be working the spell while we were down there. But this changes things."

"More like it gives you an excuse not to be with us," Cordelia said snidely.

"Are you suggesting that I don't want to help you?" Betty snarled.

"No, I'm suggesting that you're afraid of the creature, same as us. You're just too chicken to say it."

Betty's eyes narrowed. "Come here and say that."

"That's okay," Cordelia crowed.

We all knew that challenging Betty was just asking for trouble. If Cordelia pushed our grandmother too far, Betty would spell her so that she'd fart out of her mouth for a week or something heinous like that.

"So it's going to be us three," Amelia said a bit too gleefully for my taste. "The sweet tea witches together again."

I couldn't help but smile at her excitement. But trouble brewed in my stomach. "So, Betty. The three of us have to catch the alligator? How? Magic doesn't work on the beast."

A gleam glinted in her eye. "I've got just the thing for you."

"What's that?" I asked, not sure if I wanted to hear the answer.

She pulled a baggie containing horse-sized red pills from her pocket. "Tranquilizers. We're going to plant some chicken pumped with these in the sewer. Soon as the alligator eats the meat, it'll be asleep within minutes. Then you can use your magic to hoist it out of there."

"So we net it," Cordelia explained at the confused look on my face, "and then lift it. We won't actually be using magic on it. We'll be using magic on the net to get it out."

"Oh," Amelia replied. "I see. It's a total workaround."

"One that should be successful," Betty said proudly. "Then you'll bring the alligator to me, along with Adam. I'll work the spell."

I nibbled my bottom lip. "He's going to know something is up as soon as he arrives."

"The three of y'all will have to hold him with your magic," my grandmother said, chin lifted defiantly. "There won't be another choice. It will take all the power you have because he's powerful, way too powerful, but you can do it. Then and only then will I be able to work the spell and change Axel back. But Adam must be in attendance. Otherwise the magic won't be broken and Axel will be stuck in the body of an alligator—forever."

And he'll continue to slip away, I thought. The Axel that I knew and loved would disappear, and his mind would be replaced with that of a beast's for the rest of his life. Tears threatened to spring to my eyes, but I bit down on my tongue, forcing them to disappear.

It didn't help anything for me to think the worst about what was going to happen. It didn't help me and it certainly didn't help Axel.

"It's going to be okay." Cordelia rubbed my arm. "We've got this."

"But we have to find a way to get Adam out there, in the middle of the night," Amelia said.

"I'll tell him that something's happened with Familiar Place," I said quickly. "That whoever broke in the first time did so again."

"I like it," Amelia seconded. "Because since he was the person who broke everything the first time, he'll be all curious."

"He'll have to check it out." Cordelia grinned like the Cheshire cat. "Adam will know that he didn't have anything to do with it, so he'll want to find out what happened."

Betty gave me a nod. "It'll work. We just need him there at the right time. Not too soon and not too late. The tranquilizers won't last forever in the alligator's system. He's a big one, and I wasn't able to get that many."

My jaw dropped. "You have an entire bagful of pills."

"These are for cats," she told me. "Not alligators."

"But the capsules are huge," I argued.

My grandmother shrugged. "Takes a lot of drugs to bring a small animal down."

Well, that made sense then.

My grandmother clapped her hands. "Let's get to work."

My cousins and I set about opening all the pills, mixing the powder with a little bit of water and then injecting that into a raw chicken.

"Do alligators smell their food?" Amelia asked. "I mean, won't this smell and taste like medicine?"

"Let's hope their brains are so prehistoric that it won't matter." Cordelia pulled up a portion of the solution and pushed it into the breast with a turkey injector. "We'll have to tie this on the end of a string and drag it."

"All of this sounds terribly dangerous," I murmured.

"Don't worry," Amelia said brightly. "You've survived being in the sewers two times. I'm sure that you'll be able to manage a third."

Her confidence in me was almost unsettling, if you wanted to know the truth. "We'll make it work," I replied, trying to sound confident, though feeling the exact opposite.

"It's going to be fine," Cordelia said. "This will be over before you know it, and Axel will be himself again. We'll have Adam thrown back into prison, and all will be righted, the way it's supposed to be."

"I hope so," I murmured.

My cousins exchanged a look. It was Amelia who spoke. "Do you know how long it took for me to find a boyfriend, someone who understood me?"

"A long time?" I ventured.

"Forever." She rolled her eyes dramatically. "But even though I had the book under my bed, waiting to be used, I still doubted that I would find anyone who could understand me."

"Even I don't understand you," Cordelia snipped.

"That's because you never tried," Amelia shot back.

Cordelia ruffled our cousin's hair. "I'm only kidding. Of course I understand you. Sort of. But anyway. What're you saying?"

"I'm saying," Amelia started, taking the injector and filling it with the tranquilizer solution, "that you've got to have faith. Without faith, there's nothing to live for, nothing to strive for. Pepper, you can't focus on the fact that Axel's trapped in the body of an alligator and his only hope is that Betty gets the spell right."

"Wow, now I feel really good," I said sarcastically.

"Like I said," she replied, "you *can't* focus on that. What you've got to think about is reuniting your baby and husband, getting them together, mending your family. That's got to be what you're focusing on, not all the bad stuff. That won't help anybody. Am I right?"

Well, when Amelia put it that way, she *was* right. "You've got great points."

"Let me hear you say it," she said. "Say, 'I'm going to win my family back.'"

"I'm going to win my family back."

"No, no, no." Amelia shook her head. "Not like that. You can't say it that way. You've got to shout it." My cousin lifted her chin, threw back her shoulders and yelled, "I'm going to win my family back." Her voice returned to normal and she smiled. "Like that. Try again."

It felt so stupid, but I tossed my shoulders as far back as they would go and I said, "I'm going to win my family back."

"Louder," she shouted.

This was beginning to get on my nerves. "I'm going to win my family back!"

"Louder!"

"I'm going to win my family back!"

She cupped one hand to her ear. "I can't hear you!"

"I'm going to win my family back!"

"What?"

I tipped my chin to the ceiling, filled my lungs with as much air as they could hold and shouted, "I'm going to win my family back!"

"Again!"

"I'm going to win my family back! I'm going to win my family back! I'm *going* to win my family back!"

By the time I finished, I was out of breath and sweat sprinkled my brow. My body tingled with energy.

Amelia clapped a hand on my shoulder. "How do you feel?"

"Amazing." The word that sprang from my lips surprised me as much as the feeling did. "Wow. Thanks, Amelia."

Her mouth curved into a shy smile. "You're welcome. Sometimes we all need to get a little pumped up. Now. Let's finish shooting this bird with tranquilizers and get on with things."

We spent another fifteen minutes on the project. In the end, that bird was so full of drugs that I wouldn't have been surprised if the alligator dropped into a slumber just by looking at it.

We tied it to the end of a rope, and Cordelia magicked up a weighted net. "This should be big enough for it."

"I agree," Amelia said. "Just one last thing." She headed over to her wedding book, shrank it with a tendril of magic and then slipped it into her back pocket. "You never know when you're going to need it."

I wasn't convinced that we'd need the wedding book on this adventure, but to each their own.

Just as we finished up, Betty entered the living room. "I've got everything for the spell prepared. Are y'all ready?"

Butterflies swarmed in my stomach, but I swallowed my nerves down. "We're ready."

"Then let's head out."

CHAPTER 25

We didn't actually head out right then and there. Betty had forgotten about Gizzy, so we wound up calling on the men to babysit her once again.

"And this time," Larkin said to Sherman after they'd arrived, "let me do the feeding."

I liked how the men were really embracing their maternal instincts. It was good.

But anyway, once Sherman, Larkin and Shoo were settled in, the four of us headed out. Hopefully this would go fast and easy. We left Betty at the head of Bubbling Cauldron Road, where she was going to set up her spell for Axel.

All my cousins and I had to do was catch an alligator.

"He's always down this way," I told my cousins. "Closer to the heart of town."

The three of us walked until we were in a good location. We levered open a manhole cover and glanced down.

"It's too dark to see," Amelia whispered. "I'll shine some light on things."

She released an orb, and it buzzed and bumbled against the walls until it stopped dropping and hovered a good three feet above the surface of the tunnel.

The three of us gasped. Directly below us, and illuminated by the light, lay the alligator.

It was snoring.

We exchanged a look. It was Amelia who spoke. "Do we drop the chicken on top of it?"

"Yes," Cordelia said sourly, "and dance it on the creature's head until it wakes up."

"It was only a suggestion," my cousin whimpered.

"I think she's right," I said. "Amelia, I mean. We wake him up with the chicken. He'll be so groggy and hungry that he'll immediately take a bite out of it."

I hoped.

"Whatever you say," Cordelia replied, sounding unconvinced.

"I'll do it." Amelia took the chicken-on-a-rope from Cordelia and slowly lowered it. "Come on, gator. Smell that and wake up."

It started to work. The creature slowly stirred, waving its head back and forth, looking for the smell.

"You've got to lower it more," Cordelia said sharply. "It can't see it. Here. Give it to me."

"I'm doing just fine," Amelia argued, yanking the rope away.

Cordelia grabbed the rope and pulled.

Amelia tugged back, harder. "I can do it!"

"It can't see it," Cordelia argued. "You're not doing it right."

Amelia gave one more tug at the same time as Cordelia and wouldn't you know it, but the rope slipped through both of their hands and plunged into the sewer. Next thing we heard was a splash as the chicken landed.

I closed my eyes in irritation. Why couldn't these two just get along? I dared glance into the sewer and, when I did, saw the alligator swallowing the chicken whole.

"Well," Amelia said proudly. "Looks like in the end everything turned out all right."

"We still have to get him up," I replied quietly. "Hopefully it won't take long for him to be knocked out."

Amelia folded her arms. "Yeah, what if we overdosed him? Wouldn't that be terrible?"

Cordelia elbowed her. "Seeing as how it's Pepper's husband, yeah, it would be."

"Oh. Sorry, Pepper."

"It's okay." I waved away Amelia's concern. "Look, he's already falling asleep."

He was. The alligator's (or Axel's) jaws were slowing as it munched on the chicken's bones. Oh, the sound was disgusting, by the way. If you ever want to be around the most chilling noise ever, just listen to an alligator break bones. That'll remind you of your own mortality very quickly.

But I digressed.

Within minutes he was sound asleep and snoring again.

"Here goes nothing," Cordelia said.

She pulled the net from her backpack and, using magic, lowered it into the tunnel and draped it over the alligator. She was able to tuck the ends under and wrap it all around, securing the creature inside. Good thing was, not once did the animal stir.

"Let's lift him." I rose and raised my hands. My cousins joined me. As they slowly lifted the gator, I sent a line of power to the manhole, widening the mouth. The earth rumbled in protest as I forced it to bend to my will. But in the end, the hole yawned open, allowing the reptile to pass through.

I returned the hole to its normal size as my cousins continued to keep the alligator aloft. I checked the net to make sure it was secure, the entire time my heart rattling in my chest as worry pulsed through me. If the pills wore off too quickly and the net wasn't snug in one place, the alligator could slice me open with its powerful jaws.

But in the end, all was right. I gave a hard nod. "Let's take him to Betty."

The three of us were deathly quiet as we walked the streets. In fact, Magnolia Cove had gone silent. It was as if we'd been swallowed up into a vacuum. Even the very air was still.

"Something's weird," Amelia finally whispered.

"I agree. Oh, wait. I forgot to call Adam."

I stopped and dialed his number. He answered immediately. "I haven't heard from you. Everything okay?"

"No, everything's not okay. The shop"—I sobbed (it was the best fake sob that ever came out of my mouth)—"it's been attacked again. I need you here. Quickly."

Before he could say another word, I hung up. "Come on," I told my cousins. "We'd better run."

We raced the rest of the way to Familiar Place, where Betty was stationed out front. But when we arrived, someone had beaten us there.

Ellen held a knife to Betty's throat. "Drop the alligator," she commanded. "Right now or the old lady gets it."

CHAPTER 26

I surveyed the situation. Betty, for as powerful of a witch as she was, hadn't moved to stop Ellen. The woman must've had more than simply a knife to her throat. She was probably also holding my grandmother with power.

"Put the alligator down," Ellen commanded again. "I won't ask a third time."

Meaning that she would cut Betty if we pushed her patience again.

Cordelia and Amelia shot me a look, and I nodded at them. "Do as she says."

They lowered the alligator as rage ran through my veins. "Why do you want him? Is this part of Adam's plan? Does he know that we're on to him?"

Ellen looked at me, confused. "What are you talking about?"

"Adam," I nearly screamed. "You're working with him."

But as the alligator touched the ground, Ellen rushed over to the creature and rubbed a hand against him.

Next thing I knew, a *swoosh* filled the night and a portal opened. Adam stepped through, looking ticked. He spotted the alligator, Ellen and us, and the first words out his mouth were, "What's going on here?"

This was it, our one chance to end this here and now. "Betty," I screamed.

I didn't have to say it twice. She placed a finger on her nose. With one nostril covered, the other one was open to unleash magic. A tendril flew from her nose and smacked Ellen back from the alligator.

"Hold her," my grandmother yelled.

"On it," Amelia shouted.

She raised her hands, and magic flew from her fingers. It wrapped around Ellen, tying her tight.

"Pepper," Adam said. "What's going on?"

"Now, Cordelia," I called out.

The two of us wound our magic around Adam, pinning him. At first his expression was one of complete confusion, but that quickly changed to anger.

"Pepper, let me go," he said coolly.

"I know who you are," I told him. It felt so good to finally be able to admit it to his face. Granted, there were two of us witches holding him, making sure that he couldn't escape, so I pretty much had the upper hand and he couldn't hurt me. But still—it felt good.

"What are you talking about?" he said. "Who I am? I'm your husband, Axel."

"That's what they all say," Amelia shot out.

Ellen was doing her own screeching, trying to tell us that we didn't know what we were doing, that whatever we thought, it was wrong, and we were going to hurt somebody. Yada, yada, yada.

We didn't listen. Of course that's what anyone from an evil empire would say. They wouldn't admit any kind of guilt.

"Pepper"—Adam's face turned deep purple in anger—"tell me what's going on. Now. And let me go."

"I'm afraid we can't do that, *Adam*," I spat.

He paused, then his expression filled with shock. "You think...oh no...you think that I'm my brother? What could possibly make you believe that?"

The way his voice had softened sounded so much like Axel...but I wasn't giving in. I knew what I knew. It was time to tell him all about it.

"What makes me believe that is that Harry from Castin' Iron saw you fix my shop at the same time that you were having dinner with me, at the house. A person can't be in two places at once, Adam. Everyone knows that...well, you can be if you're using dark magic. But Axel would never do anything like that. So I called Witcheroo and you know what, they couldn't find you. The guard I spoke to said that Adam—*you*—was gone. I'm not stupid. You escaped, came to Magnolia and turned Axel into the alligator so that no one would find him. Well, we're going to turn him back. That's what Betty's working on right now."

The blood in Adam's face drained away. "No, Pepper. You've got it all wrong. I'm Axel. I didn't want to tell you, because I've been trying to find a way to fix it myself, but I don't know how." He glanced down at the magic holding him, and when he looked up, his eyes brimmed with worry. "Something's taken control of me. I've been cursed. It's a splitting curse. It causes me to split into two and be at two places at once."

"Likely story," I sneered.

"I'm telling the truth." His voice broke. "If I don't stop it, it will kill me!"

His words sent a barb to my heart. I took a few hesitant steps toward Adam.

"Please," he begged. "If Betty tries finishing this spell, it could kill me. Axel isn't the alligator. I've been right here, all along."

I stared up into his eyes—eyes that it felt like I'd known since my birth. Well, not since then, really, but our connection was so close that Axel always was my other half.

I reached out to him telepathically. *Axel?*

He smiled. *I'm right here.*

My eyes narrowed. *I tried contacting you the other night but you didn't reply.*

Was that the night I fell asleep after you gave me that heart-stopping sugar cake? I can't talk when I'm asleep.

I scowled. *You knew what it was?*

Of course. He smirked. *How could I not?*

Oh no. What had I done? "Cordelia! Let him go. It's Axel. I've been wrong. All wrong."

Cordelia released her hold on him. But I had to stop Betty. If that alligator was only just an alligator and it wasn't tied to anyone, she could kill Axel.

I whirled toward her. "Betty!"

But she was head-deep in magic. Literally. Power swarmed around her, forming a cocoon. It was thick and deep. Betty's eyes had rolled into the back of her head, but she kept chanting.

I grabbed Axel's hand. "We have to stop her."

"She's too caught up in it," he ground out. "If we jolt her now, she could blow up all of us. There's too much power."

He was right. Magic buzzed all around. It lifted the hair on my arms, even raised the hairs on my head. The very atmosphere hummed. Like gas filling a house, all the magic needed was one spark and we'd be blown to bits.

"She's going to kill him," Ellen yelled.

The alligator?

"Betty," I screamed. "Betty, stop!"

But she couldn't hear me. She was tangled up in her spell, oblivious to all of us. She wouldn't come out of it until her chanting was over and the spell was ended.

What could we do? We had to wake Betty up without shocking her. She would need to retract the magic slowly so that it could weaken and fizzle out on its own.

But how? She was so encapsulated that I couldn't see a way in.

Then I had it. "I know what to do." I kissed Axel's cheek. "Hold my hand and don't let go."

He nodded solemnly, aware of what my plan was. "Be careful."

I closed my eyes and reached for her. *Betty! Betty, can you hear me?*

It took a moment, but finally I heard, *What?*

She sounded muffled, just like she did whenever we talked on a cell phone. Of course, that was because she held them upside down.

Am I clear to you?

Yes, Pepper. What do you want? I'm kind of busy.

Really? This was how she was going to act? *You've got to stop the spell. The alligator isn't Axel. Adam isn't here. I was wrong.*

I can't stop, she replied, her voice sounding strained. *He's tied. The alligator is enchanted.*

What? That can't be.

It is. The spell is working. I can feel the tether.

Oh, my gosh. The truth had been right in front of me the whole time, but I'd been too blind to see it. *Betty, turn the spell to Ellen.*

Huh?

Just do it. Trust me.

I could sense her hesitation. *Are you sure?*

I'm sure.

I opened my eyes and turned to Axel. "She's going to finish the spell."

Alarm filled his eyes. "Why?"

"Because there's more going on that we didn't see."

It was so obvious now, and it surprised me that I hadn't seen it before. But of course I hadn't realized it, because I'd been so distracted by everything else.

Let me explain—I'd only ever seen Ross during the day, and I'd only ever seen Ellen at night.

But wait, that wasn't entirely true, was it?

I'd seen Ellen one day, had in fact spoken to her. But she hadn't looked like Ellen. She'd been that little bird who'd told me not to harm the alligator.

That had been Ellen, and every night I'd seen her hanging around the sewers was because she was protecting her husband, Ross.

By day, Ellen was a bird and by night, Ross was an alligator. They'd both been enchanted, or more like cursed, for some reason.

But that curse was hopefully about to be broken.

As I thought all of that, Betty's spell was strengthening. Her magic wound around the alligator and then Ellen. Betty's voice crashed against the very buildings, made the trees sway, shook my eardrums—such was the power of the spell she was wielding.

"Hang on," Axel yelled. He took me in his arms and threw up a shield to keep us from blowing away.

Cordelia and Amelia also threw up shields in order to remain safe.

A great *crack* filled the night. Then, just as quickly as the power had flared, it was done.

The night became still once more. I blinked my eyes open and saw, to my delight, Ross lying in the net where the alligator had been.

Amelia released her hold on Ellen, who, tears streaming from her eyes, raced over to her husband and threw her arms around him, crying.

Axel quickly magicked up clothes for a very naked Ross (not that I noticed), and we unwound him from the net.

He hugged his wife and smiled at us. "A witch who was jealous of our love enchanted the two of us so that we could never truly be together. Ellen would come out of her bird form just as I was turning into mine."

"We'd come here every night," Ellen explained. "So that Ross wouldn't hurt anyone. We thought this would be the perfect town to survive in, but the animals in your store distracted him."

Ross nodded. "Even in my animal state, I hated seeing other creatures penned up. So I'm the one who broke your store."

Oh. My heart cracked a little at that. My store hadn't been destroyed out of malice. Ross had been trying to save the animals. He'd had enough consciousness to think that harm was going to come to the puppies, kittens and others who would become familiars. And he'd wanted to save them.

So he'd trashed the place and broken the glass. Ellen explained that she worried for the creatures, so she took all of them away to keep him from going back.

"Thank you," Ellen said to me. "I'm sorry for earlier, but I thought that you were going to hurt him."

"We only wanted to help," I told her. Axel placed a hand on my shoulder. I slid my own over his, luxuriating in his warm touch. "We were a bit wrong in our theory, but it all worked out in the end."

She smiled. "And I bet you're wondering where your animals are."

My eyelids flared in surprise. "Yes, I am."

She grinned from ear to ear. "I'll take you to them."

CHAPTER 27

It turned out Ellen had been keeping the animals not far away at all, in an old abandoned house. She'd been visiting them twice a day and had been feeding them.

Ellen explained that she didn't release the potential familiars because she was afraid Ross would just wind up breaking into the store again. But with both of them cured, there was no fear of that.

"Thank you," she told me again when I retrieved my animals.

"You're very welcome," I'd said.

She had also confessed that Ross had placed the alligator suit in the tunnels so as not to be discovered. Just went to show that folks would do whatever it took to keep their secrets safe.

I was back at Familiar Place and had just returned the animals to their spots and had canceled the order for more creatures when the door opened and Axel walked in.

I cannot tell y'all what a relief it was to know that I had my husband back. Or, well, that he'd never gone anywhere to begin with.

"Looking good," he said proudly, placing a Styrofoam box on the counter.

I couldn't keep the glee from my voice when I asked, "Oh, what's that? It smells heavenly."

"Barbecue." He winked. "And a slice of chess pie."

I crossed over and wound my arms around his neck. "You treat me too well."

"To be honest, I'm glad to have my wife and daughter back at the house. It was weird for a few days there."

"You mean when I thought you were going to steal our child?"

He rolled his eyes. "That. But anyway, I called the prison."

"And?"

"Turned out, what you received was a miscommunication. The day you called, they were moving Adam into another portion of the prison, so he wasn't on the regular roster. He'd been giving them a hard time, and so he was being relocated."

"So that explains why the guard said he'd left."

Axel shrugged. "Not really. But what's done is done." A dark expression flitted across his face. "It's time to move on."

I recognized the worry that unfurled inside him. "Tell me what happened."

He shook his head. "I don't know. One day I felt fine, and the next, everything was off. I could feel myself splitting, like I did that one day. It hasn't happened since, and I don't know why. But there's only one explanation as to what happened—someone's cursed me. The person who's cursed can become twinned, though it doesn't usually last a long time. What Harry saw was a shadow of me. By now, it should have vanished. The curse also makes me forget things, things that I should know."

Which explained why Axel had forgotten where Cordelia worked.

But he kept going. "Eventually, the magic will kill me."

Fear jumped into my throat. "Maybe you're wrong."

Axel shook his head sadly. "I'm not wrong. From everything I've read, that's what's occurring."

I grabbed his arm, looking for a lifeline in the sea of uncertainty. "But there's got to be a way to stop it."

Axel shook his head. "There is none."

"I don't believe that. I *can't* believe it."

"You have to believe it. We've got to enjoy what little time we have left because soon I'll be driven mad, and after that will come death."

My heart ached. My entire body tensed with fear and worry. I would not let anything happen to Axel. Whoever did this to him was going to pay. I would find them and we would fix this.

Or I'd die trying.

∽

Pepper's adventures continue in SOUTHERN TRAPPINGS. You can order it HERE.

Be sure to sign up for my newsletter so that you never miss a release. Click HERE to sign up!

Plus, join my private Facebook group, the Bless Your Witch Club. There you will receive sneak peaks at books, be the first to receive special giveaway offers and watch as I interview other authors that you love. But it's only available in the club, so join HERE.

And…I love to hear from you! Please feel free to drop me a line anytime. You can email me amy@amyboylesauthor.com.

ALSO BY AMY BOYLES

SERIES READING ORDER

A MAGICAL RENOVATION MYSERY
WITCHER UPPER
RENOVATION SPELL
DEMOLITION PREMONITION
WITCHER UPPER CHRISTMAS
BARN BEWITCHMENT
SHIPLAP AND SPELL HUNTING
MUDROOM MYSTIC
WITCH IT OR LIST IT
PANTRY PRANKSTER
HOME TOWN MAGIC

LOST SOUTHERN MAGIC
(Takes place following the events of Southern Magic Wedding. This is a Sweet Tea Witches, Southern Belles and Spells, Southern Ghost Wrangles and Bless Your Witch Crossover)
THE GOLD TOUCH THAT WENT CATTYWAMPUS
THE YELLOW-BELLIED SCAREDY CAT
A MESS OF SIRENS
KNEE-HIGH TO A THIEF

BELLES AND SPELLS MATCHMAKER MYSTERY
DEADLY SPELLS AND A SOUTHERN BELLE
CURSED BRIDES AND ALIBIS
MAGICAL DAMES AND DATING GAMES
SOME PIG AND A MUMMY DIG

SWEET TEA WITCH MYSTERIES

SOUTHERN MAGIC

SOUTHERN SPELLS

SOUTHERN MYTHS

SOUTHERN SORCERY

SOUTHERN CURSES

SOUTHERN KARMA

SOUTHERN MAGIC THANKSGIVING

SOUTHERN MAGIC CHRISTMAS

SOUTHERN POTIONS

SOUTHERN FORTUNES

SOUTHERN HAUNTINGS

SOUTHERN WANDS

SOUTHERN CONJURING

SOUTHERN WISHES

SOUTHERN DREAMS

SOUTHERN MAGIC WEDDING

SOUTHERN OMENS

SOUTHERN JINXED

SOUTHERN BEGINNINGS

SOUTHERN MYSTICS

SOUTHERN CAULDRONS

SOUTHERN HOLIDAY

SOUTHERN ENCHANTED

SOUTHERN TRAPPINGS

SOUTHERN GHOST WRANGLER MYSTERIES

SOUL FOOD SPIRITS

HONEYSUCKLE HAUNTING

THE GHOST WHO ATE GRITS (Crossover with Pepper and Axel from Sweet Tea Witches)

BACKWOODS BANSHEE

MISTLETOE AND SPIRITS

BLESS YOUR WITCH SERIES
SCARED WITCHLESS
KISS MY WITCH
QUEEN WITCH
QUIT YOUR WITCHIN'
FOR WITCH'S SAKE
DON'T GIVE A WITCH
WITCH MY GRITS
FRIED GREEN WITCH
SOUTHERN WITCHING
Y'ALL WITCHES
HOLD YOUR WITCHES

SOUTHERN SINGLE MOM PARANORMAL MYSTERIES
The Witch's Handbook to Hunting Vampires
The Witch's Handbook to Catching Werewolves
The Witch's Handbook to Trapping Demons

ABOUT THE AUTHOR

Hey, I'm Amy,

I write books for folks who crave laugh-out-loud paranormal mysteries. I help bring humor into readers' lives. I've got a Pharm D in pharmacy, a BA in Creative Writing and a Masters in Life.

And when I'm not writing or chasing around two small children (one of which is four going on thirteen), I can be found antique shopping for a great deal, getting my roots touched up (because that's an every four week job) and figuring out when I can get back to Disney World.

If you're dying to know more about my wacky life, here are three things you don't know about me.

—In college I spent a semester at Marvel Comics working in the X-Men office.

—I worked at Carnegie Hall.

—I grew up in a barbecue restaurant—literally. My parents owned one.

If you want to reach out to me—and I love to hear from readers—you can email me at amyboylesauthor@gmail.com.

Happy reading!